AND IT HAPPENED IN
BEAUMONT STREET

Edited by

Heather Gelles Ebner

BOMBUS BOOKS
15 Henleys Lane, Drayton OX14 4HU
www.bombusbooks.co.uk
www.fast-print.net/store.php

ISBN 978-178456-466-7

A catalogue record for this book is available from the British Library

First published 2017 by
BOMBUS BOOKS
an imprint of Fast-Print Publishing
Peterborough, England

Disclaimer
And it Happened in Beaumont Street is fiction. Although it is based
on many well-known places around Oxford any reference to living
individuals is accidental

Acknowledgements

The editor, authors and publisher would like to thank the Ashmolean Museum for providing the cover design and graphics for this book, and for selling it through the museum shop. Some of these stories relate to the Ashmolean's collections and its Head of Publishing, Declan McCarthy, has helped ensure they are factually correct.

In acknowledgement of this support, all profits from the sale of And it Happened in Beaumont Street are being donated to the Ashmolean Museum.

Oxford Inc.

Andrew Bax was once a publisher and spent much of his life issuing deadlines to busy professionals who had very little time for writing. Now that he writes himself he wonders why none of them, as far as knows, blew a gasket

Janet Bolam's birthday falls on May 13th. For dramatic effect, she sometimes tells people it was also a Friday, although it wasn't. She recommends the ploy as a great way to start a conversation with strangers

Geoff Bremble, a native of Wirral, ventured south some 35 years ago and then spent 20 years working at what is now Oxford Brookes University. He currently entertains himself with golf, gardening and supporting Tranmere Rovers Football Club, as well as penning short stories and a larger one where he explores his Irish ancestry

Jenny Burrage belongs to three writing groups which all meet in Oxford. She was delighted when the editor of the Oxfordshire Limited Edition magazine asked if she could publish one of her stories. Fame at last!

Heather Gelles Ebner lives in Oxford with her husband, two boys and a hamster. An expat from New York, she's learned to love the rain and queues but is still working on Marmite

Neil Hancox has contributed to seven or more anthologies and three e-books; a few years ago he won first prize in a Ramblers Holidays travel writing competition. He often walks along Beaumont Street though so far none of the adventures described here has befallen him

Jackie Vickers has had many different and interesting occupations but now prefers to escape into imaginary worlds of her own making

Annie Winner has mostly been interested in life writing, and experimenting with fiction is a new venture. It allows her to test the theory that you should never let the truth get in the way of a good story

Contents

Introduction

HEATHER GELLES EBNER

Ask any Oxford native where to find Beaumont Street and expect a puzzled look. There follows a delay of a few seconds before he or she replies vaguely, 'I think that's the one that...' We can forgive them for not remembering since, being home to several of the city's iconic buildings, the name of the street is rarely necessary. People are better off simply asking for directions to the Ashmolean Museum, the Randolph Hotel or the Playhouse, for example – and often do. It's tempting to wager that almost every journey to Oxford involves at least a few minutes in Beaumont Street, whether to visit these notable venues or simply to get from north to south by car. It is practically the only way through the city given its pedestrianised centre.

Like other Oxford streets, such as Broad, High and Turl to name a few, Beaumont Street offers a rich history and, of course, a wonderful source of inspiration for the imaginations of a small group of writers, Oxford Inc.

This collection of short stories spans the present, the past and even the future. The delicate thread that ties them all together is this much beloved street. Sometimes it isn't the 'when' that is fascinating, but 'where'. Like a geological survey of this city street, story by story its character and characters are revealed. Peel back a layer, take a peek and enjoy. Whether tragic or comic, imagined or real on the pages that follow; it all happened in Beaumont Street.

Going for Gold

JANET BOLAM

"*An inquiry is being held into the death of Arnold Soffier (49) who was found hanged in his cell in Kynton Cross Prison early on Tuesday morning. Soffier, reputed to be the leader of the gang who carried out the 2001 Great London Vault Robbery, has always protested his innocence. Krugerrands worth over £50 million were stolen in an audacious heist on August 18th 2001. Just £5 million has been recovered, the rest is believed to be hidden by members of the gang.*"

It may seem illogical after all these years, but I jump every time the doorbell rings, especially when it rings and rings … and rings, like it did the day I heard about Arnie. I rushed upstairs and peeped out of the window to see Dylan McKane. A bit worse for wear, but definitely him. I sat on the edge of the bed trying to catch my breath. What the hell was he doing here? By the time I summoned up the courage to return to the window, he had moved away from the door and was pacing along the front of the house, looking for a way to break in. That figured.

'Nice to see you again, Bet.'

'Serena. I changed my name.'

'No shit? Serena?' Dylan laughed out loud and I remembered why I used to find him so repulsive. 'Serena Soffier?'

'Pearl. Serena Pearl. You shouldn't be here, especially today. Wasn't that what we agreed?'

'I never agreed to anything.'

I watched him ladle four sugars into his mug of tea.

'Why've you come?'

'To express my condolences on the untimely death of your brother-in-law.'

'Thank you.'

'There's no way Arnie took his own life,' Dylan continued, his eyes not leaving my face. The teaspoon grated as he stirred and stirred. 'He was murdered. He was murdered in his cell in cold blood by someone who wanted information from him.' He took his tea to the window and peered sidelong down the street.

'Are you being followed or something?' I could hardly stand the tension.

'Just being cautious, that's all.'

He threw himself into the armchair, tapping his foot with a nervous impatience.

'I only just heard about your old man. I'm sorry. He was a good bloke.'

Nick, my wonderful husband, had a heart attack five years ago, and died. I relive that day every morning when I wake up and every night when I go to sleep. He was my angel and I miss him beyond words. But you've got to carry on with life, haven't you? Dylan was still talking.

'I've been travelling a lot since I got out. I had to keep on the move until Interpol got bored, and then I went on a roundabout route to Quito.'

'Quito?'

'Via Berlin and Amsterdam.'

'Quito?'

'Yes. Big mistake. Some of it was still there, but only some of it. The thieving bastards strung me out.'

So that was the reason he was here. He was out of money. Dylan was a last-minute member of the gang when Arnie and Martin thought they might need a bit of muscle, just in case. I remember Nick was dead against him joining us, but he was outvoted.

'And what about you?'

'Spent, years ago. We never had much of the share in the first place.' I managed a nostalgic sigh. 'More tea?'

As it happens I had been living well, but never flamboyantly, on our share of the money. Until today, I'd managed to nurse myself into a feeling of security. After all, Nick was released without charge, innocent as the day is long as far as the cops were concerned. However, Dylan's appearance could blow the roof off that one, especially now, when the robbery was in the news again. There was no getting away from it, Arnie's murder had brought me a heap of problems. Dylan cracked his knuckles and began pacing again.

'There's some murdering bastard out there who knows where Arnie's money is. We've got to get to the money first, Bet. You and me. Let's face it, Arnie's got no use for it where he's gone, now has he? You tell me where it's hidden and we'll share it, right?'

'But I don't know where it's hidden.'

Dylan stopped in his tracks and swirled to face me. He pulled up a chair, pushing his face into mine. 'Are you sure you haven't any idea where it is, Bet, 'cos if you do, you'd better remember, fast.'

A chill ran through me. I knew what Dylan was capable of.

'Not a clue,' I levelled eyes with him, 'and anyway, we're probably too late. If the murderer did find out, then wouldn't he have collected it already?'

'If the murderer was an inmate then he'd have to make arrangements with someone on the outside - or wait until he got out himself.' Dylan cracked his knuckles again, went to the window to repeat his sidelong glance. 'It's a race against time. You'd better remember something, fast.'

'Like I said, I know nothing.'

His patience snapped, he grabbed my arm tight and growled 'Don't lie to me. Not to me. I know you visited him. What did you talk about?' I knew that if I showed him any fear, I'd be done for.

'He's my brother-in-law, so of course I went to visit him, quite a few times. It would've looked suspicious if I hadn't! But why would he tell me anything? He was expecting to be out after his next parole.'

'I don't know why, Bet, but I'm not convinced.'

'Back off Dylan! I don't know where the money is – I'd tell you if I did, because believe it or not, I don't want Arnie's murderer to get it either.' He considered this a while.

'But you may want to keep it all to yourself, and that wouldn't be fair, now would it? Not at all fair.'

'You're wasting your time.' I continued with the righteous indignation for as long as I dared, but I was chancing my luck. Before I could defend myself he had his arm round my neck.

'You're right. I haven't got time to mess about. Those big blue eyes of yours don't fool me. You know where he hid it and you're going to tell me.'

I could smell his sweat, I could feel him shaking. I had to

think of something fast.

'Martin!' I managed, 'perhaps Martin knows?' Martin was the fourth member of the gang. We called him the Accountant because he was the one with the knowledge and connections in the world of finance.

'Martin? He's disappeared.'

'I know where he is! I can ring him. He – he might know something.'

'I need more than that.' He shook me as if by doing so more information would rattle out.

'He – he visited Arnie, I know that they talked about investments...'

'What sort?'

'Please, Dylan! That's all I know.'

He released me.

'Phone him. Tell him to get his arse over here, but don't tell him I'm here.'

Martin could hear the tone of my voice. He's a clever boy, is Martin.

'He'll be here, but it has to be tomorrow. He's in the Turks and Caicos, but he said he'd come...'

Dylan wasn't happy, but he settled down in front of the TV and turned on the racing.

'I wouldn't mind a bite to eat. Got any bacon?'

My Nick worked at the Oxford Playhouse, down on Beaumont Street. I used to call it his Other Woman because he was always there, and if he wasn't, he'd be thinking about it. It was his job to look after everything to do with the building. He made sure that every show was helped to 'get in' smoothly and 'get out' on time, whether it was a big touring company or a small amateur group. He had a cool head on his shoulders, and was very good with his hands. Very good. He knew about the heating, the air con, the plumbing, the electrics, where all the damp patches were. He often rolled up his sleeves to carry out some maintenance or another instead of calling in a contractor. Nowadays it wouldn't be allowed, but those days, that was how it was. Not much money and much less regulation.

When he died, I didn't know what to do with myself. I imploded, as they say, but eventually I had to pick myself up and be practical. I became a volunteer usher at the Playhouse just to feel connected to him – and it also solved certain practical problems I was facing.

After the robbery, Nick and I had the small problem of how to disappear £65 million worth of Krugerrands. A tube of 25 1oz Krugerrands is three inches long and weighs a pound and a half. Nick and I had 400 of the little buggers to hide, and although it only amounted to the volume of 17 average house bricks, each one weighed 38 lbs, so handling large volumes was a problem not of size, but of weight. Nick got creative and fashioned lots of ingenious hiding places around the Playhouse, small but able to take the weight. He was so clever. Unless you knew exactly where to look, the chances of finding them were remote, even for a professional. So you can immediately spot how important it was for me to continue to go to the theatre after my Nick passed away, and why I needed access to areas well beyond where the audience could go. Over the years I developed ways of accessing the stores, taking one tube out at a time. Luckily, I could easily tuck the odd tube into my handbag, and each tube held £25,000 worth of Krugerrands, so not a bad day's work. Martin had created a financial set up to convert the

Krugerrands into 'pounds, shillings and pence' and to move it to an account in the Turks and Caicos Islands. It was a well-oiled machine. Like I said, Martin is a clever boy.

I watched Dylan wolf down a whole packet of bacon, three eggs, four pieces of toast and the remains of my bottle of sherry, which took the edge off his mood. It was then I told him I had to go to the Playhouse that evening. Of course he said I couldn't go, until I explained that the front of house manager had arranged a small leaving party for me in the bar after the show. That got his attention.

'Leaving?'

'I know, but I've been volunteering there for nearly five years and I think I need to move on now.'

'Where did you plan on going?'

'I'm not going anywhere. I just don't want to volunteer there anymore. But, look, if I don't turn up tonight my friend Marcie'll be very worried and she'll be straight round knocking on the door to see if I'm alright.'

I waited an anxious minute or so as the slow cogs in Dylan's brain turned.

'I'm coming with you' he eventually growled, 'I'm not letting you out of my sight.'

After the break-in, they took all the gold to a lockup in Luton so they could parcel it out. Then each of them had prepared hiding places, but before Arnie had a chance to hide his share, he was picked up by the police - a sticky wicket if ever there was one. His gold was still in the lockup and it wasn't a safe place to leave it. Nick got to work in the Playhouse and we moved all the gold there. We bricked it in under the stalls, all safe and ready for Arnie to collect when he got out.

Using the Playhouse to hide our money and Arnie's was always a risk. If Arnie did crack and told his murderer where his Krugerrands were, it didn't just expose Arnie's money, it told them where mine was too, and I still had ten tubes there, worth £250,000. My priority had to be to get the rest of my own money out of the Playhouse. I could have done without Dylan. How was I going to get them out of the Playhouse without Dylan noticing? I could fit them into my sturdy bright red Cath Kidston handbag, but could I carry 15 pounds in weight in a way Dylan wouldn't notice? And even if I could get them home, how could I hide them from him? It would be like carrying seven bags of sugar. In the end, I took a tote bag and swung it nonchalantly on my shoulder all the way to Beaumont Street, hoping for the best.

The theatre was buzzing. I took my place inside the door to the stalls, and Dylan took his station a few feet away, beer in hand. He never took his eyes off me. Not for one minute. The play was very moving, the sort where, at the end, the audience sit as one body, silent, before breaking into wild applause, and rising to deliver a standing ovation. The kind of play that gives theatre a good name. All of this was lost on Dylan, of course. The audience lingered longer than usual, stopping to chat in both bars. This was good. The longer the building took to empty, the better.

'Still got work to do,' I chirped and set off upstairs to the circle bar; Dylan followed close behind like a persistent bulldog. I headed for the corporate loo. I call it the corporate loo because it's one of two on the first floor, next to the room they hold corporate functions. Very nice, with proper walls from floor to ceiling and a nice, lockable door.

'I'm popping in to have a pee. You can come if you like, or

you could sit in the bar. Up to you.' I tried to keep my voice light.

Door locked, I got down to business. I quickly removed the carpet and detached the floorboard beneath. I reached down the hole and unhinged a disused drainage pipe. One by one, I took the tubes out and stuffed some into my tote bag. I decided I could carry eight of them. Not easy, but do-able.

My leaving party was sweet. We had it in the circle bar. There was bubbly and cake and the front of house manager, who remembered Nick, made a small speech about how the place would never be the same again, and my friend Marcie made everyone laugh with a poem about me. Dylan attracted a few interested looks as he sat nursing yet another pint, so I whispered to Marcie that he was a friend of Nick's brother. She raised an eyebrow, but that was about it.

Perhaps it was my nerves, or the glass of Prosecco, but on the way home I realised there was no way I could carry the tote bag to the bus stop on St Giles, it was far too heavy. We needed to get a taxi. I leaned hard into the heel of my shoe and thank the living Lord, it snapped off. I made a huge fuss limping about on the pavement, declaring I couldn't walk anywhere with a broken heel and anyway, I may have sprained my ankle. I refused offers of a lift (I didn't want anyone else involved in case things went wrong) saying it was OK, we'd get a taxi and, right on cue, one drove by. I staggered into my seat leaving Dylan no choice but to follow me.

Finally home, Dylan found my bottle of Jack Daniels and poured himself a generous glass. I suggested he sleep in the guest room. Dylan laughed as he pushed the sofa to the bottom of the stairs.

'I'm not stupid Bet. I'm kipping right here. And besides, you aren't my type, love. Now Nick, he was definitely my type…' and he slumped on the sofa leaving me to clamber across it and him, and upstairs to my room, with me clutching the tote bag as casually as possible.

I lay on my bed, listening for signs of Dylan. Was he asleep? Was he still drinking? I heard the sound of the TV, and I must have dropped off. Somewhere around three in the morning I heard loud banging. Dylan, very drunk, was turning my living room upside down.

'Where's the money, you little bitch? I know you know where it is!' he roared. He raced upstairs and kicked open my bedroom door.

'Is it here? Have you got it hidden here? I'm not stupid.' He was so drunk he hardly knew what he was doing. He emptied drawers, pulled all my clothes out of the wardrobe, ripped open the mattress. I shrank into the corner, and watched as my tote bag got buried deeper and deeper under bedding and the contents of my chest of drawers. Finally he stopped and staggered downstairs. I crept to the top of the stairs and watched him as he snored, splayed out across the tatters of the sofa. The TV was still playing. I sat on the top step, waiting for the morning. Suddenly, he was wide-awake. We both were. The BBC early morning news was broadcasting.

"*Reports are coming in that the Oxford Playhouse was ransacked in the early hours of the morning. Video footage shows an unidentified lorry parked up against the backstage door at 3.30 am and leaving at 5.15 am. The backstage areas have been ransacked, leaving the auditorium and the bar areas undamaged. We will bring you more on that story later in this bulletin.*"

Dylan narrowed his eyes. I held my breath as he began to nod, like it was all beginning to make sense to him.

'I've got business to deal with, Bet, and then I'm coming back to deal with you, you lying bitch. Don't try to hide, 'cos I'll find you.' He tottered to the sink and vomited. He left before Martin arrived.

'Everything alright?' Martin asked, surveying the damage ruefully, picking his way past the upturned sofa. 'I took the trouble of popping into the Playhouse before I came here. The place is swarming with police, and they've cordoned it off. Quite hard to get in, actually.' He paused for dramatic effect. 'It's still there. The stalls are untouched.'

I broke down in tears of relief. The gold was safe, and Martin was here. He pulled me close and kissed me.

'Let's leave it there for now. We've plenty to be getting on with. We'll collect it when the dust settles. Come on, let's get this lot tidied up, and be on our way.' He pulled out a passport from a neat briefcase.

'Yours, I believe, Serena Pearl.'
I looked at my new passport, my new identity, my new life.

'Don't bother packing. We'll just get you clothes at the airport. Got the petty cash?'

'In my tote bag,' I replied.

Eight months later on our small island retreat, waves washing the golden sand of the private beach, our tranquillity was disturbed by a small report on the BBC Oxford website. The Oxford Playhouse was to be closed for the summer for a complete refurbishment. There's no peace for the wicked, is there?

Flambé

ANDREW BAX

This was meant to be a love story. It has all the right ingredients: a beautiful girl, a besotted companion – attractive more for his wealth than for youth or good looks but attractive all the same – and a romantic escape to the city of dreaming spires. It could have turned out so well...

It was a bright but chilly morning in early Spring as a coach load of Chinese tourists sped along the M40. This was the second day of their 'Europe in a Week' holiday and already they were exhausted. Yesterday had been the Tower of London, the London Eye, the British Museum, Harrods and *Les Misérables*. Today they had already done Windsor and would soon be in Bicester Village; they then had two hours in Oxford before travelling on to Stratford and the Royal Shakespeare Theatre. Tomorrow was to be the Shakespeare Tour and Birmingham Airport before flying to Paris and Disneyland; a packed itinerary of European cities was to follow.

A yellow Lamborghini roared by. It belonged to Piers, a name as new as the car. Until recently he had been just plain Peter but that didn't seem in keeping with his transformation from a lowly position in the family firm to full-time playboy. Whereas Peter was modest and retiring, Piers was fast learning how to become an extravagant extrovert. Peter had inherited the business but instead of reviving its fortunes, as everyone hoped, he promptly sold it and set about spending the resulting millions. And he became Piers.

His suit was replaced by expensively ripped jeans, his tie by designer sunglasses hooked into the top of his shirt. Everything about him had designer branding and he attracted a new set of designer friends. He was intoxicated by their hedonism. Pretty girls, whose names he hardly knew, flocked to join him in expensive clubs and restaurants. There was stiff competition to be seen in that yellow Lamborghini as it prowled the streets of Mayfair, Kensington and Chelsea, radiating testosterone.

One of the prettiest girls was coming with him to Oxford. Her name was Carmen. Not her real name, of course, but one that blended well in the exotic circles she frequented. If asked, Carmen would say that she was a model, or a fashion editor. Both occupations attracted her in an abstract kind of way but she hadn't yet found the time for them. Besides, her father's allowance hardly made it necessary. She didn't really know Piers but he seemed fun and spent his money freely. He was also intriguingly unattached. Some suggested that his real preference might be for pretty boys but Carmen doubted it. She intended to find out.

Ahead of them, in one of Oxford's most famous kitchens, that night's dinner was in preparation. For a popular item on the menu, cubes of prime beef were being marinated in a good Merlot with paprika seasoning. Named after a diplomat in the court of Alexander I of Russia, the original recipe first appeared in print in the 1871 edition of the classic cookbook, *A Gift to Young Housewives*. This was a Russian equivalent to *Mrs Beeton's Book of Household Management* and it went through several editions before the Bolsheviks banned it as bourgeois propaganda. The wave of refugees fleeing the Revolution introduced the recipe to many other countries, where it was adapted to local tastes, and it became particularly popular in China. Whether any of the Chinese tourists now in Bicester Village were familiar with the dish is unknown. They were busily engaged in filling suitcases with discounted fashions, many of them made in China.

The Lamborghini growled into Beaumont Street and drew up outside the canopy that crossed the pavement. From road to roof the car was just 44 inches high and, as Carmen discovered, getting out could not be achieved easily or elegantly, particularly when wearing a short, tight skirt and high heels. Piers slipped the concierge £20 to park the car and take their luggage to Room 405, recommended because of its quiet seclusion at the top of the hotel. It was time for lunch and he had set his mind on Browns, a favourite of his student days.

Carmen hadn't been to Oxford before and, so far, was unimpressed. All she had seen was a load of old buildings and she was beginning to wonder where the shops were. However, over the speciality burger and salad Piers talked wistfully and amusingly of beer and parties and friends with whom he had lost contact, remembering sometimes to ask Carmen about herself, and she told him about other parties and other friends.

After lunch they wandered towards Worcester College from where Piers, then Peter, had scraped a pass degree in organic chemistry. They clambered up dark, steep staircases and paid homage to a locked door barring entry to the room Piers had occupied for a while. They visited the dining hall, the chapel and library. They strolled round the gardens, Piers still talking, Carmen thinking about shoes, and stopped to admire the magnolias, now in billowy full bloom. Then, instinctively, as they walked back up Beaumont Street, they held hands. Piers was enchanted by her youth and sparkle – and Carmen? Carmen was determined to have a good time.

Room 405 was secluded alright, and was reached along narrow, winding corridors, up flights of steps and down more, but it had a nice view overlooking the entrance to the Ashmolean Museum. It was on the small side, occupied almost entirely by a king-size bed, and Piers was tempted to ask for something grander. While he was thinking about this and gazing out of the window, Carmen went to explore the bathroom. She emerged a few minutes later wearing something small and lacy, a twinkling little smile, and nothing else.

Contrary to popular belief, the hotel is not named after the colourful Lord Randolph Churchill, father of Sir Winston. He was a mere lad of 15 when the hotel was opened. It is, in fact, named after the Randolph Sculpture Gallery in the Ashmolean Museum opposite. However, Lord Randolph often dined in the hotel when he was at his country residence, Blenheim Palace. He is credited with the particular version of the dish still marinating in the kitchen, having complained that the original recipe was too bland. It was he who suggested spicing it up, and the new recipe became so popular that it was largely unaltered for over 100 years.

It is reasonable to assume that Carmen's appearance and her soft arms, now encircling Piers' neck, her warm body pressed to his and her heady fragrance would combine to ensure a predictable sequence of events. But Piers needed to be prepared for this sort of thing. He had learned from previous experience that without being suitably fortified with a nice wine, and perhaps a whisky, disaster would ensue. He started to panic. He and Carmen had been getting along so well and now the silly girl had spoiled it all. If she could only have waited until after dinner, everything would have been fine. Instead he was standing helplessly in Room 405, in the middle of the afternoon, stone-cold sober. Carmen skipped into the bed.

Memories of previous disasters came flooding back. Something soft hit him in the face. It was small and lacy, thrown at him by its owner, now jiggling her toes in excitement and fluttering her eyelashes at him over the top of the duvet.

This wasn't the time to look again out of the window but, had he done so, Piers would have seen an open-top bus disgorging a party of Chinese tourists who obediently followed their guide into the Ashmolean. Like a man condemned, he slowly unbuttoned his shirt.

In the Randolph Sculpture Gallery the guide was doing her best to bring life and meaning to the broken torsos on display. They made little impression. Neither did the mummies and other artefacts from Ancient Egypt. There was a flicker of interest in the early Chinese paintings and carvings, but her party hadn't come all this way just to look at that kind of stuff. Only when they reached the museum shop did they become animated. Looking anxiously at her watch, the guide went to round up the stragglers and told the others to wait for her outside. This was an opportunity for selfies with Henry Moore's *Three Piece Reclining Figure* in the background.

In the kitchen the marinade was drained; the beef was patted dry and dusted with flour, mustard, salt and pepper. It was fried in smoking hot oil until brown and a ladle of brandy was added, igniting with a satisfying whoosh of blue flame which disappeared up the ventilation shaft. In another pan, shredded onion and mushrooms were sautéed in butter until soft, then some beef stock was added. It was left to simmer until reduced, when crème fraîche would be stirred in.

Things were not going well in Room 405. Piers and Carmen were now occupying separate sides of the bed, an icy gulf between them. Carmen had never felt so angry and humiliated and couldn't wait to tell her friends *everything*. Fears that she might do exactly that dominated Piers' concerns. Both of them were also wondering how they could get out of the bed with dignity and escape back to London alone.

These thoughts were interrupted by the realisation of something strange happening in the room. It wasn't a sound; the light didn't change but there was definitely *something*. They both sensed it at the same time, then they sniffed and sniffed again. Smoke.

Meanwhile in the kitchen Maris Piper potatoes were being sliced into thin strips and dropped into a tub of cold water; later they would be dried, deep-fried and served as matchsticks.

Suddenly, alarms were ringing. There were shouts and sounds of running. Someone pounded on the door of Room 405 before unlocking it with a master key to find its occupants hastily getting dressed. Outside, the first fire engine arrived, followed by several police cars. In what seemed to its

Chinese spectators like a well-rehearsed routine, both ends of Beaumont Street were cordoned off and suddenly there was no traffic. Instead, the road was filling with people rushing out of the hotel, while burly fire fighters rushed in. Two more fire engines arrived; there were more ladders, more hoses, more police. Smoke was beginning to seep through the roof. Soon a jet of high-pressure water, aimed by a man on a hydraulic platform, was seen to be pouring into Room 405.

On the far side of the road Carmen's nimble fingers worked speedily on her smartphone. Soon howls of laughter erupted around the globe as her Facebook friends read of that afternoon's events, and saw a red-faced, tousle-haired Piers being interviewed by police seeking witnesses. Oblivious to this little drama, the party of Chinese visitors had a grandstand view of the fire from the terrace of the Ashmolean. Later they would agree that it was the highlight of the entire trip.

BBC News Bulletin, 14 April 2016 *The £6.5m renovations at a five-star hotel in Oxford damaged in a major blaze have been completed. The fire at the Randolph Hotel in April 2015, sparked by a flambéed beef stroganoff in its kitchen, ripped through three floors. Manager Michael Grange said he was proud the 150-year-old building was back to its former glory. He said staff had been 'particularly outstanding' during the 'difficult period'. Beef stroganoff is no longer on the menu, he added.*

Letters from Beaumont Street

JACKIE VICKERS

16 Beaumont Street
Oxford
Tuesday September 3rd 1895

My Dear Edith,
I have been in Oxford for little more than a day but I already feel quite refreshed. I think Aunt Vera rescued me just in time. Mother was furious that I should be missing Mrs Cadwallader's garden party for she cares only about the invitations I get. She has complained a lot about Aunt Vera, saying she reads too much and ignores the benefits of society and furthermore is convinced she harbours suffragist tendencies. She also said that Aunt Vera wore herself out doing those business translations when she could have been going out in society, and she only has herself to blame, if she is still unattached, as she had plenty of offers. But honestly, Edith, Aunt Vera doesn't look at all worn out and was as excited as I was when the train arrived at Oxford station.

But you asked me to tell you about Oxford, though there's not much to say yet, except that all the buildings look splendid and somehow stately. Aunt Vera says I must expect to walk a great deal if it is fine, as there are so many parks and water-meadows, but I shall not mind if it rains and we are kept indoors, as so many people walk up and down Beaumont Street, I could sit at the window for hours. The Ashmolean Museum is at one end opposite the Randolph Hotel, which is much bigger than the Railway Hotel at home, and Worcester College is at the other. Beaumont Street itself is quite wide with rows of creamy stone terraces with attractive balconies.

Your loving friend, Maude

PS Two young ladies have just gone past on their bicycles, wearing the latest in cycling outfits and no-one stared at them as they would have at home. Aunt Vera says it is a common sight in Oxford.

16 Beaumont Street
Oxford
Tuesday September 3rd 1895

Dear Mother,

Our rooms are very comfortable and our landlady was most welcoming. Her maid Tilly looks after our every need, from breakfast on a tray in our rooms, to posting this letter, so you need have no concerns over my well-being.
It was overcast today with frequent showers, so we hurried to the Ashmolean Museum, which is just at the end of this street, for Aunt Vera has a particular interest in their collection of Minoan pottery.

Please give my love to Father,
Your loving daughter, Maude

Wednesday September 4th

My Dear Edith,

There were some heavy downpours today, but Aunt takes no notice. We picked up our skirts and ran down the road to the museum. You would never think Aunt Vera was nearly 29!

The director of the Ashmolean made his reputation with archaeological digs on the island of Crete, where he uncovered an entire civilisation. Aunt Vera is very keen on archaeology and has read a great deal about Sir Arthur Evans' discoveries of the Minoan culture. Mother has written, complaining that I do not write about anything interesting. She is very keen to know what the ladies in Oxford are wearing, which does not interest me at all!

I have just learnt that our neighbour here in Beaumont Street is none other than Mr James. Mr Henry James! Tilly told me when she brought breakfast this morning. She had been gossiping with the maid from next door, who told her the rooms had been let to a famous writer. I told her the plot of *The Portrait of a Lady;* you will remember that it made me cry so much last year. But Tilly said she would never cry over people who had that much money, so I didn't tell her about any more of Mr James' books, as they are all about rich people. Apparently he goes to the Randolph Hotel for tea every day, as a great friend of his is staying there.

Your good friend, Maude

16 Beaumont Street
Wednesday September 4th

Dear Father,

Thank you so much for the money order and your recommendations to spend it on cream cakes and ribbons. I have determined to buy a book for Aunt Vera to thank her for all her trouble. I know she likes Henry James and has not yet read *The Tragic Muse*. There are many bookshops here and I daresay I shall be tempted to treat myself too!

Your grateful, and loving daughter, Maude

Thursday 5th

My Dear Edith,

You asked for exciting news and here it is. Aunt Vera suggested tea at the Randolph Hotel as we might get a glimpse of Henry James. We were lucky to sit at the next table and had a very good view of him. He is a bit portly and balding, but has very twinkly eyes and smiles a lot. His friend was French! I have never seen a Frenchman before, though Aunt says if I looked about me I should see a lot of foreigners in Oxford. This man attracted a lot of attention from hotel staff and visitors. Aunt put it rather well, she said his voice resonated, which was a polite way of saying he was noisy and made a fuss. Actually it was a good thing because we were able to learn a lot about him. He is Monsieur Paul Bourget, who was made a member of the French Academy last year, which Aunt says is a great honour. His wife is his secretary and looks quite worn out and didn't eat a thing, even though the cream cakes were wonderful. I noticed both Mr James and his friend were eating copious amounts. It is a pity M. Bourget talked so much, as I should have liked to hear what Mr James had to say. Aunt Vera says we should come again, as hearing the conversation of great writers is very instructive and an opportunity not to be missed.

Your friend, Maude

Beaumont Street
Friday 6th September

My Dear Edith,

As we were leaving our lodgings this morning, who should come out of number fifteen but Mr James! He turned towards us, raised his hat and wished us good morning. He is quite reserved, yet has a wonderful warm and friendly smile. 'Fancy being acknowledged by your favourite author,' I told Aunt Vera. After we had walked round a good deal, we made for Blackwells, the booksellers opposite the Sheldonian Theatre. Aunt told me that when they first opened, about fifteen years ago, there was just one tiny room and now there are three, all bursting with books. While Aunt was upstairs, M. Bourget came in, enquiring in a loud voice whether his latest book was on the shelves. Mr James was hovering outside. I should think he was embarrassed, he seems quite a shy man, so I slipped out after him. 'Excuse me,' I said, 'I know we have not been properly introduced, but I am staying at number sixteen Beaumont Street.' 'Ah, yes, the young lady and her aunt,' he said with a little bow. (How did he know? Tilly I suppose.) And I took courage from this and told him how wonderful I found *A Portrait of a Lady*. I told him that Aunt loves his books and I had just bought her *The Tragic Muse* and asked if he could possibly sign it. 'I am touched by your enthusiasm,' he said and took the book. 'I shall drop it in at your lodgings.' I saw Aunt peering out of the doorway and excused myself. 'It has been a pleasure,' he said, and raised his hat. Just think! I shall be able to tell my children some day, that I spoke to Henry James. Now what do you think of that, Edith?

Happily yours, Maude

16 Beaumont Street
Friday September 6th 1895

Dear Mother,

I hadn't realised you expected me to write every day and I am sorry to have disappointed you. We walk a great deal here. Yesterday we went down the High to Magdalen Bridge, we spent an hour in the college chapel, had tea and a bun in a teashop nearby then crossed into the Botanic Gardens where we spent the whole afternoon. We came back along Long Lane, Holywell Street and Broad Street, which, I think you will allow, amounts to a lot of walking. We then partook of a light supper and went to bed early.

Your dutiful daughter, Maude

Friday 6th

My Dear Edith,

Mother has written to complain that I do not write every day. Apparently she had made this a condition of my going away. She wants to know every detail about those aspects of life which do not interest me at all such as: are the clothes freshly laundered and does Tilly have clean hands? She hopes our landlady wears sober colours and removes her apron when she comes up to speak with us. She also says I must not walk so much as I may exceed my strength, whatever that means. And I am to write to George, now that he is back at school, as he is eager for news about his sister. He never wrote to me from Scotland, but I am to set him an example, 'being two years older, and being a girl'.

Today we went for a long walk through Christ Church Meadow and along the river bank and on to Christ Church Cathedral. We were feeling very tired, so Aunt proposed tea at the Randolph again, to revive our spirits. The tea-room was packed, I don't know why there were so many visitors today. Mr James, who was there with his friends, caught sight of us looking for a table and came across to beg us to join them. I suppose he sees we are enthusiastic devotees of his work. Madame Bourget has a beautiful oval face, but looks rather frail. Her husband is not very tall and very dapper in his dress. He has smooth pomaded hair but a straggly moustache. I could feel M. Bourget looking at me quite a lot. He asked if we had visited Worcester College and said the gardens were particularly delightful at this time of year and perhaps he could show us round. I must say his wife looked rather bored, perhaps she is not so fond of gardens as he is.

Aunt Vera said that would be delightful, but then Mr James said regretfully he had to be in London for a few days, and I saw Aunt Vera's face fall. He has started writing for the theatre. I wonder if he will be as successful as a playwright as he is a novelist.

I hope you are not bored by all this detail, but meeting famous writers is not something that happens to me very often!

Your devoted friend, Maude

16 Beaumont Street
Oxford
Saturday 7th September 1895

Dear Mother,

How kind of Hubert Vaughan to invite me to join their family for the Hunt Ball. I am sorry you accepted on my behalf before I had the opportunity to discuss it with you.

Maude

Saturday morning

Dear Edith,

Something awful has happened! Mother has accepted an invitation from Hubert Vaughan for me to join their family for the Hunt Ball. Did you ever meet him? He has receding hair and will inherit the family business. He took me down to dinner at the Richardsons. I thought we were having a perfectly normal conversation about Liberal foreign policy, over the soup, when Hubert said 'I didn't know young ladies were supposed to have opinions on such matters' and he turned to speak to Muriel Thoresby who has absolutely no opinions whatever! So I can't see why he invited me, unless Mother had a hand in it and has started match-making already. A year to find someone, a year engaged and married by twenty. Aunt Vera saw how upset I was, for she told me that I should not feel I have to go. Even in her day, girls could refuse invitations.

We are having luncheon with a friend of Aunt's who has her own business. Aunt does Italian translations for her. She wants me to meet someone who has become happy and successful while keeping out of the marriage market.

You are so lucky having parents with advanced views.

Ever your friend, Maude

16 Beaumont Street
Oxford
7th September 1895

Dear Mr Vaughan,

How very kind of you to invite me to the Hunt Ball. I am so sorry that Mother accepted on my behalf. She was unfortunately unaware that I have agreed to my Aunt's suggestion that we should visit Italy this autumn.

Yours sincerely, Maude Stanhope

16 Beaumont Street
Oxford
Sunday 8th September 1895

Dear Mother,

As you will see from the enclosed copy of my letter to Mr Vaughan, I have refused his invitation. I would beg you to discuss any further invitations with me before accepting them on my behalf.

Maude

Sunday

My Dear Edith,

I hardly know how to tell you what happened today. At the last minute Aunt said she felt unwell and did I mind meeting the Bourgets without her. But when I got there, M. Bourget was on his own! He said his wife was exhausted as she had spent the morning copying out his work and didn't seem to mind that Aunt had not come. He knows Worcester College gardens very well and had even written about them and suggested we sat on a bench by the lake. The gardens were just about empty, which was just as well as M. Bourget took out the book he had written, called *Sensations d'Oxford* and began to declaim in a very theatrical manner, in French! You know what my French is like. I only caught a few words and then they didn't make sense. He kept repeating: 'Oh! Une femme qui ne parlerait pas…' He saw my confusion and translated. It was all about wanting a female companion who was beautiful but silent. Which I think is most insulting

- don't you? I asked if we could walk around the garden (knowing he couldn't walk and read). He put his book away and said it would be cool under the trees and taking my elbow steered me into the deep shadow of some old oaks, whispering compliments all the time. Then he took my hand and leant forward to kiss it. Imagine my discomfort! Fortunately it was fairly dark under the tree and we were quite alone. As he had already made his preference clear for a silent companion, I decided to pay him back by talking endlessly, which I did right through the gardens and up to No 16 Beaumont Street! That evening I told Aunt Vera all about the episode in the garden and made it clear that I had in no way encouraged M. Bourget. She laughed till she cried and congratulated me on spoiling his little idyll. Then said I must on no account let Mother ever find out or she would never be allowed to take me anywhere again.

I'm glad my little adventure in the garden made Aunt Vera laugh, as up till then I had felt the afternoon was wasted. The gardens really are beautiful and I would have much preferred enjoying them on my own. In silence!

Yours, amused, Maude

16 Beaumont Street
Oxford
9th September 1895

Dear Mother,

I am sorry you are so upset by my letter to Hubert Vaughan. It is better that I should refuse his invitations rather than give him any hopes of my interest in him.

You may rest easy about Italy. Aunt Vera has no intention of going. I thought it seemed like a legitimate excuse as I know of several girls of my age, whose fathers are in business, who are to visit Italy in the coming year.

There is absolutely nothing I can tell you about whether lilac or lemon is the preferred shade for this autumn. Women in Oxford seem to me to be entirely taken up by the beauty of the buildings and by the quality of the cream cakes. It is possible that the fashionably minded go to London.

Your obedient daughter, Maude

Monday 9th September

Dear Edith,

Aunt tells me that Mother has written to explain, yet again, that she intends me to make a good marriage and this cannot be achieved if I become too cerebral. Evidently she would rather I walked around gossiping about clothes than went to museums and looked at all the wonderful buildings.

Aunt says sometimes you have to get away in order to understand things about yourself. Certainly the episode in the garden with M. Bourget has clarified much for me. I have no intention of becoming one of those silent women he (and Hubert Vaughan) so admire. I have never before considered studying at a university, as everybody I have ever met seems to think education is wasted on girls. However, I have talked long with Aunt about university entrance requirements. She thinks I may not be too far from the expected standard and suggests I come to stay with her to study with a couple of tutors she has in mind. Neither of us knows yet how to approach Mother, or whether to try Father first.

We leave Oxford tomorrow. It has been quite an experience and I am now ready for the fight. For there will be a fight! I shall come and see you as soon as I have discharged those obligations which Mother expects of me.

Your devoted friend, Maude

On hearing of the death in Venice of his great friend the writer Constance Fenimore Woolson, Henry James visited Mrs Phillips at No. 15 Beaumont Street and arranged to take Miss Woolson's old rooms for a few weeks where he wrote the short story 'The Altar of the Dead'. *At the same time Paul Bourget was enjoying an extended stay, with his wife, at the Randolph and the two friends would meet every day for long walks about the city. Paul Bourget wrote* Sensations d'Oxford *(published in 1891) while living in rooms in Walton Street. In the section on Worcester College gardens, the narrator does indeed express his desire for a beautiful, but totally silent female companion. Miss Woolson's death was explained as an accident by her family, but accepted by most as suicide at a time when she was feeling especially depressed.*
Leon Edel's biography of James gives further information on James' relationship with these two writers.

The Stanhope family are entirely fictional. However, Maude's longing for further education and possibly even employment outside the home was typical of many middle-class girls in the late 19th century.

A Little Discretion

H G EBNER

It would just have to do.

Ordinarily, he would have gone to London for this kind of work. It warranted the expertise of top specialists. But that could be a rather protracted affair and, under the circumstances, he simply hadn't got time.

Alasdair Duncan-Smith glanced over his shoulder as he passed the windows of the Randolph Hotel. No one he recognized in the tea room. In a place as small as Oxford, the risk of bumping into someone he knew was not insignificant, and he was determined to keep this visit to Dr Fielding's office completely clandestine. Alasdair was not a good liar, so he walked briskly and cast his eyes nervously about. The very idea that he might have to explain what errand he was attending to on Beaumont Street made him sweat. Pausing beyond the Playhouse, he turned to face the block of pale stone buildings opposite and waited for the stream of cars and bicycles to pass. Then Alasdair furtively dashed across. He mounted the steps in front of the bright red door of Number 27 and pressed the buzzer.

'Dr Fielding's office,' a cheerful voice rang through.

'Alasdair Duncan-Smith,' he whispered, 'from the College.'

'Oh yes, he's expecting you. Come right upstairs, second door on the left.' A buzz and a click, the door unlocked and Alasdair hastily pushed through.

Following a thorough examination, Dr Fielding faced Alasdair with a rather grim look. He sat behind a great leather-topped desk, his chin pinched between thumb and forefinger. Still thinking. Fielding took off his spectacles and laid them on a pile of books and papers. 'I have to be honest. This might be beyond my ability to help.'

Alasdair looked ashen.

'And,' Fielding continued, 'if I *do* help, I can't offer a lasting solution. It's a patch job at best. You do realize this, and you still wish to proceed?'

Alasdair nodded without hesitation.

From the window, slightly ajar, he could hear people and cars on the street below. It was nearly noon. *The streets will be even busier now*, he thought with increasing discomfort. The probability of someone recognizing him was rising exponentially.

'I must tell you, the bone is shattered in so many places that it's practically imposs...,' Fielding trailed off. Desperation stared at him, pleading. 'I do appreciate the situation you're in.'

'So then you'll do it?' A glimmer of cheer had returned some colour to Alasdair's cheeks.

'To be clear, if it were anyone other than you, Alasdair, I wouldn't even consider such an... well, unorthodox procedure.' Fielding tapped the desk lightly with both hands. 'Very well, I shall see what I can do.'

'Before next Friday?'

'Bit of a squeeze. But yes, I shall find a way to fit this in.'

Alasdair stood, visibly relieved. He shook Fielding's hand energetically and gathered his coat. As he opened the door to depart, Dr Fielding called out.

'I will have to replace the missing fragments. Chimpanzee bone might be the best we can do. I assume that's alright?'

Back in College, Alasdair climbed the worn wooden steps of Staircase 12 to his tiny office overlooking the quad. He switched on his computer. An email message from the Master, Lord Hughes, was awaiting response.

`'How's the patient?'` the Master wrote.

Having broken a priceless treasure, the Master still managed to find humour in the situation. He'd even touched his nose conspiratorially when Alasdair proposed that a quiet visit might be in order this time to a conservationist on Beaumont Street known for his discretion.

Not only had the Master got tipsy, or rather, tipsier than usual, at the guest night dinner, but after dropping and shattering the priceless early hominid skull, he had kicked broken shards under the carpet. Hiding the evidence or his embarrassment, it was hard to guess what the Master had been thinking. Alasdair sorely wished that he'd at least thought to mention it *before* the cleaners came through the next morning. By the time he learned of it, any fragments that experts might have reaffixed (albeit with painstaking effort) had been hoovered up, dumped in a bin and were already on their way to landfill. It was nothing short of disaster.

The Master, however, greeted the fiasco with his usual relaxed confidence. He possessed the calm, untroubled air of a man who's spent a lifetime occupying rather rarified social status. Someone else would always sort things out.

Lately, that was Alasdair.

As the College Archivist, Alasdair was responsible for recording and writing about his illustrious Oxford College's history, more than eight centuries of it. But he was also responsible for the more prosaic tasks; rescuing 16th century manuscripts from years of damp, restoring crumbling parchment maps, arresting decay on original wax-sealed deeds, and cleaning or repairing any priceless objects that might become damaged. Of which there seemed to be a great many, since the arrival of the Master, Lord Hughes.

The Master was a great enthusiast of the College's archival treasures. He loved showing them off, nearly as much as he loved showing off the College's wine collection. Unfortunately, these two passions did not mix well. In spite of Alasdair's gentle protestations, Lord Hughes insisted upon displaying rare historical treasures whenever an opportunity presented itself, which rather unfortunately tended to coincide with the unrestrained consumption of fine Claret. There was the Annual Feast honouring their patron saint, the Old Members' Gaudy, any occasion at which a member of the Monarchy was present, and guest night dinners when a major benefactor was invited to high table – particularly if said benefactor was an American.

'History is of little use locked away in a cupboard, Alasdair! Come now, let's give the *[insert valuable artefact]* a good airing!' Lord Hughes would say with a wink and a jolly pat on the shoulder. 'That ought to impress our former Colonists, eh?! This relic is older than their entire country!'

Alasdair had lost track of the precise number of 'incidents' but a few were simply unforgettable. Like the time the College's original land deed went missing, only to be discovered coated in a thin film of beer following a rowdy pub quiz. The Master had felt it necessary to settle a heated dispute between himself and an Old Member from the Class of '57 over the College's founding date. Or worse, the time a glass of Burgundy somehow upended itself all over the single most valuable page of a Matriculation Register, the one bearing a certain Prime Minister's signature at the tender age of 18. Why had the Master opened the glass cabinet in which it was safely displayed? With a full bloody wine glass in his hand?! You simply didn't ask.

The Master, affable and ruddy-cheeked, found his mishaps rather baffling. He could never satisfactorily explain how they occurred (though a good accounting of port bottles illuminated most mysteries) but, to be fair, he never blamed anyone else. Still, his obvious proneness to accident failed to curtail his zeal for prying College treasures from the safety of their cupboards. Much to Alasdair's chagrin.

Dr Fielding's concerns were well justified.

Piecing together shattered bone was not an easy task. Even for an expert. But replacing all those missing shards, that was the rub. It would be rather tricky, delicate work and, given the time constraints, chimpanzee bone would have to suffice. It was certainly unorthodox but there was nothing else for it.

It was an ancient skull after all. One couldn't just pick up *Neanderthal* bone fragments on eBay. Well, not from reputable sources anyway. There were ways of obtaining this material or, where appropriate, making plaster casts for a faithful reproduction. But the Master wanted the skull by the end of the week for a guest night dinner. Besides, who would notice the difference?

The cranial bowl had been used to serve chocolates, for as long as Alasdair could remember, in the more intimate setting of the Senior Common Room to which special guests and the senior fellows withdrew after formal dinners. It was quite the conversation piece. He had first seen it as an undergraduate. Invited by his History tutor to join the fellows after dinner, he'd been completely mesmerised – the heavy velvet drapes, animated faces flickering in the glow of candelabras, and the chocolates nestled inside an ancient skull. It was undeniably atmospheric.

The fragile skull was the first of the College's treasures that Alasdair researched when he took up his post as Archivist many years later. It came into its possession sometime in the 1860's when the Geology professor (a famed anatomist and fossil hunter) returned from a dig in the Far East. Long before regulations required one to declare such finds or compelled one to leave them in the country where they were found, the professor had pluckily brought three sets of bones back to England. Two of them, forming complete skeletons, had made their way to appropriate homes – one in the British Museum and one in comfortable storage at the Pitt Rivers just down the road. But the third set of bones, being incomplete, made it no further than his office in college. Where they remained. With no heirs, all his papers, books, and a veritable cabinet of curiosities from his adventures were bequeathed to the College when he died.

Though difficult to pinpoint whose idea it was, sometime in the early 1920's mention of 'unexpected delights' and a skull-shaped bowl appeared in college records. As far as

Alasdair could tell, the skull had been in service ever since. It was the sort of detail the Guardian would love to bang on about but not many outside a few VIP guests and professors had ever seen it. Sure there were the odd rumours, occasional speculation, but no one in the College ever officially confirmed these for fear of inspiring some undergraduate reporter to agitate for repatriation, ceremonial re-burial or some other perfectly reasonable but inconvenient idea.

By Friday morning, Alasdair was getting cold feet. He could not shake off a feeling of unease. Attempting to pass off a jigsaw puzzle of human and chimpanzee bones held together by Henkel's adhesive as an ancient hominid skull now seemed a decidedly bad idea. What began with good intentions as a Make Do and Mend now felt like the greatest hoax since Piltdown man. What if someone noticed? But, try as he might to persuade the Master that rushed repair work might be imprudent, Lord Hughes could not be moved.

'Have a sherry old boy, settles the nerves.'

'The thing is,' Alasdair cleared his throat, 'we could simply get a proper restoration done instead of making a hash of it. I mean, rushing it. We'll have to do that anyway – eventually?'

'Alasdair,' said the Master, 'how many guest night dinners have taken place on the sixth week of Hilary term since 1920?'

'Ninety six.'

'And at how many of them have we served chocolates from that skull?'

'I'm not certain, early records are patchy, but probably ninety three, ninety four?'

'Precisely. That's nearly a century. We can't change it now – just isn't done. For Heaven's sake, are you forgetting that last year we paid an absolute fortune (and I had to dip into my own pockets, I don't mind telling you) to procure a certain port just to ensure we serve the same vintage that we have been pouring since the Queen's coronation? Incidentally, she's touched by the gesture.'

'But,' Alasdair tried, 'we could use the silver salver. The one given to us by...'

'Not on my watch,' the Master cut him off. 'You change one detail, where does it end? Oxford abides by its traditions, no matter how inconvenient they may be. That's the point. Good God, we don't want to end up like the Americans! Nothing's sacred over there. It's all singing, all dancing – ghastly. Which reminds me, I've got an email waiting from our venture capitalist.' He raised his eyebrows mischievously. 'Made a pile since he was here as a lad. I've got a good feeling about this one – let's give him a show!'

'Shall I at least alert a few of the Fellows, just in case?'

'In case of what? Don't over think this. A little discretion never hurt anyone. He's a venture capitalist, not an appraiser from Sotheby's. Be a good man and pull that door closed on your way out, won't you?'

Alasdair embarked on the second of his clandestine journeys across town in less than a week. He took the long way this time, walking first toward the train station and then doubling back to Beaumont via Walton Well Road. He was eating antacids like sweets and could not wait to have this whole sordid business behind him. With a little luck, Fielding's repair work would go unnoticed. As long as the Master's guest was suitably impressed with the evening's post-dinner theatre, it would all be fine. By the time anyone capable of noticing such discrepancies was invited for future guest night dinners, the skull would have been sent to London for a full and proper restoration. What was needed right now, was precisely what Dr Fielding offered.

A patch job.

'Here you are. It's not my best work but at least you have it in time for dinner this evening.' Dr Fielding gestured toward the small hat-sized box on his desk.

'I can't thank you enough,' Alasdair said, taking the box and placing it in his satchel. Fielding waved the compliment aside with modesty.

'Don't thank me until you've had it properly restored. That was one hell of a job, Alasdair. I've had to use adhesives that, frankly, would be deemed 'recklessly damaging' by some of my peers, but needs must. I've also given it a tea bath to disguise the newness of the replaced bone, but it isn't as dry as one would like. Keep it away from the Master's water glass.'

Alasdair sighed wistfully; if the Master ever drank from his water glass they wouldn't be in this predicament.

'Duly noted. And thank you again. I wouldn't have asked this of you but it can't be helped. You know how it is. Tradition,' he shrugged apologetically. 'This evening's guest is rather important. The Master's PA has been trying to get a date in the diary for more than a year. Timing is everything with these venture types. Seems we're within sight of a very significant benefaction. Anyway, one wants to impress,' Alasdair rambled, 'he's never dined at high table before.'

Dr Fielding nodded lightly, 'Yes, well, good luck tonight.' He pinched his nose where his glasses rubbed. 'Alasdair, do me a favour, will you? When you do send it for proper repair later on, don't tell them who worked on it.'

Alasdair understood. He scurried down the stairs, out of the door and hurried back to College as inconspicuously as possible. Drinks would be served in just over an hour.

By all accounts, dinner that evening went brilliantly. The hall was splendid, filled with liveliness, students in black tie and gowns looking their best, and the Chef outdid himself. At high table, conversation flowed easily, as did the wine. The Master appeared to be on form. He and his American venture capitalist were getting on like a house on fire. He could hardly wait for the *piece de résistance* that awaited them once they retired for coffee, chocolates and port.

To the bang of a gavel, and a closing Latin prayer, the Master and fellows rose, ushering their high table guests toward a small adjoining room. The Senior Common Room was a much quieter affair; seated at the dining table bathed in candle-light under the approving oil gaze of the great and the good from bygone eras of college history. Feeling positively ebullient after the capitalist's overtures of philanthropic support, the Master leaned back and signalled the butler to *bring the chocolates.*

The moment had arrived.

Two stewards returned to the room, one bearing a bottle of port and the other carrying, in white-gloved hands, the skull. Cradled inside the fragile treasure was a small green silk pillow bearing twelve chocolate truffles. Lord Hughes nodded to his right – the chocolates should be served first to his guest of honour. The American's face said it all – marvel and surprise confirmed the object had had its desired effect. Thoroughly satisfied, the Master could at last turn his attention to other pressing matters. He had detected the absence of a port bottle to his left where it ought to have been, if Fellows and guests were passing it round properly. Feeling antsy, he would have to take measures, but with charm; these things must be done delicately. He made cursory conversation with the guest on his left for the first time that evening.

'I'm afraid we've not yet had the pleasure of conversation,' the Master began. 'Have you travelled far?'

'Yes, I've just arrived from Beijing.'

'Aha, jet lag! You must be too tired for port,' the Master offered in commiseration, his eyebrows hinting at the bottle which had halted its perambulation around the table. Catching on, the guest pushed the bottle toward the Master with an apology.

'So, what brings you to our fine college this evening?' the Master continued as he poured himself a tiny glass.

'Professor Johnson. He has invited me so many times but I am always in the field and away for long stretches. Never seem to have time to get to Oxford.'

The Master, contented and ruddy cheeked, addressed Professor Johnson. 'Tsk, tsk. A last-minute guest with no proper introduction?' He wagged a finger, gently ribbing. 'But never mind, I do like a bit of mystery,' the Master chuckled. The steward captured his attention and offered the chocolates, which he declined with a pat of his colossal belly. He gestured magnanimously toward the jet-lagged academic guest beside him.

'Can we tempt you with chocolate? Not to be missed here,' he winked.

The skull and chocolate truffles were presented.

The Master carried on making small talk but paying little notice. He was distracted by the progress of port which had once again slowed at the far end of the table. 'Delighted that Professor Johnson's persuaded you at last...' he muttered. 'What did you say your line of scholarly endeavour is?'

'Paleoanthropology.'

'Ah yes, jolly good,' the Master said, failing to hear. At last, he'd caught the eye of the fellow delaying the port and visually hurried it along.

'And, Professor Johnson tells me that the college has always wanted an expert opinion. It is my honour to be able to identify this enigmatic skull for you. May I?' he asked the Steward, taking the delicate cranium into his hands and inspecting it with reverence.

The Master's left eye began to twitch. 'What's that now? Er, yes, quite – we have always wondered...' he spluttered.

A hush fell on the room. Now stiflingly hot, the Master flapped his ceremonial robe for air. The venture capitalist looked on with interest as the wide smile of the paleoanthropologist faded to a quizzical expression, turning the skull in his hands. 'Uhm...'

Pity. It had all been going so well.

The Messiah

ANNIE WINNER

She's late. I've been sitting in the Drawing Room at the Randolph Hotel for a good ten minutes wondering about every woman who walks in. Is that her? I've never met her or seen her performing but her agent had assured me that I couldn't miss her. She would be carrying a large orange handbag. He was right – there she is. I half rise from my seat to catch her eye. We shake hands and my knot of irritation at being kept waiting is immediately dissolved by her show-stopping smile and apologetic warmth. 'Sorry', she says. 'My train was late, the traffic awful and I had to dump my stuff upstairs'. She sinks elegantly into her chair, kicks off her shoes and we order tea – Earl Grey for her and a herbal for me.

As a freelancer I'd jumped at the commission from a Sunday colour supplement to do this interview, although with some trepidation. A lot could ride on what I made of this chance. I knew from the research I'd done that she'd grown up in a council estate on the edge of the city. Little mention is made of her personal life in her Wikipedia entry apart from her marriage to Thomas Devine, the music critic, and the births of their three children. The rest is mostly a list of the recordings made, the prizes won, and that she lives with her family in Birmingham. Facebook and Google yield little more than her musical life.

I don't know anything like enough about music to engage with her on that. What I'm after is the personal angle – the life behind the public persona, what makes her tick and how she got to where she is, a top classical violinist at the peak of her career. I switch on my digital recorder. I'm nervous. Her agent had mentioned that she doesn't often agree to be interviewed.

My first question does not go down well. I wonder how staying at the poshest hotel in Oxford feels, a rags to riches question. 'I get asked that kind of thing all the time,' she says, with a trace of belligerence. 'I feel what anyone from my background would feel – intimidated, out of place, anxious – but also entitled and a bit angry. I bet you wouldn't ask Nigel Kennedy that question.' I kick myself for not thinking of a better opener. I realise I am fishing in murky waters.

I try a different tack and ask how she manages to be away from home, sometimes for weeks on end. I wonder how working so often in the evenings impacts on her family life, mentioning my own mother's struggles with the conflict between career and family. She looks slightly startled at this question. She says it's not something she's been asked before and laughs when I joke that no one would ask Nigel Kennedy such a question. She talks of the toll the conflicts took, especially when her children were tiny. She'd worked so hard to get where she is but had wanted a proper family as well, and juggling the two was as hard as it is for anyone. She says it isn't so bad now they are all at school, but even so, if she wants to keep her career she still has to practise or rehearse for several hours every day. She has to be out in the evenings at least two or three times a week, often a long way from home, and away on tour several times a year. So how does she do it? 'I really don't want to talk about my private life,' she says, but with her bright smile warming her words, 'but I can reveal' – she giggles – 'that I have a husband who knows how to be two parents in short bursts, who mainly works from home, and – when the kids were tiny – we had a wonderful part-time nanny'.

She pauses, now looking wistful, then reflects on how often she's had to miss bedtimes, school events, and family occasions like birthdays and anniversaries. I wonder whether she thinks the children suffer from her absence. She says, 'How can we know that? They don't know any different. They seem OK and Tom is nearly always there and when he isn't his Mum will step in'. She turns the question back on me. 'You mentioned your mum worked hard. So did mine. That's normal for us. How can we know what difference another way of life would have made? No one worries about men whose work means being away from home a lot.'

'Are any of them musical?' I ask, not entirely innocently – this might be a way in. She talks a bit about her middle child who is doing well on the oboe. The other two are less enthusiastic but she jokes that they have little choice other than to soak up playing and listening to music as part of the life their parents lead. I spot my chance to cast my line a bit further and ask whether she comes from a musical family. Her face clouds over and I let the silence lengthen. On my recording you can hear the murmur of the other voices in the room, the brittle chinky click of cups on saucers providing a soundtrack for the tension of that moment.

Eventually she draws a deep breath. It transpires that she knows very little about her father. Of course she'd asked her mother Jean about him, but she was a woman of few words anyway and clearly didn't want to talk about it. She'd only provided the skimpiest information. He was 'foreign' and she'd met him through the church she attended. He sang in the choir and had gone back to his country of origin not knowing what he'd left behind. I want to ask her if she would like to track him down, to know him, but something stops me. She's flowing along now with little prompting from me, describing how her mother had brought her up alone with the help of her own mother who'd lived with them until she died in the late 1980s. Jean had had no particular interest in music – her priority was to earn a living. For much of her daughter's childhood and adolescence her night job, cleaning shops in the Cowley Centre, put the food on the table. It paid the rent, the utility bills, the bus fares, the mainly charity shop clothes, the occasional cinema trip, but not a lot more. Jean would get home at around 7 am and then at times would work all morning at another job in Littlemore. She would then salvage a few hours sleep until school finished. There wasn't room for much else in her life.

Jean had done her best to understand her daughter's ambitions and always tried to be in the audience for school concerts. She made sure she wasn't distracted from doing her homework and smoothed over complaints from the neighbours, about the sounds of her practising through the thin walls of their flat in Windrush Tower, with the occasional cake. The neighbours on the other side kept a watchful eye when Jean was at work. 'I always felt my mum was on my side, even though she couldn't share what I was starting to experience. For her, life was a struggle to make ends meet, to find ways of getting a good bargain and affording things that most people take for granted. We never had a holiday or a car or even a meal out.

When I ask how her talent had been discovered she describes her primary school where in those days they provided taster classes in various instruments. If anyone then wanted to take it further they were set up with a teacher and could hire an instrument. She's never forgotten that first session, when she drew the bow across the strings, groping for the note. Next came the feeling of satisfaction when she found it – alone in the group. Miss Herman, the music teacher, nodded at her approvingly and soon had her marked down as a definite candidate for further lessons. But how could her mum afford them? It was out of the question. She'd slunk out of the room when Miss Herman wasn't looking. The next day Miss Herman made sure they bumped into each other. She quickly grasped the problem and within a couple of weeks she'd phoned to say she'd applied to a local music charity for funding for both lessons and the hire of the instrument, and a month later they heard the bid had been successful.

Quite a story, I think, feeling like a fisherman trying to keep the line taut enough to draw the catch in but loose enough to keep it swimming. She is looking quite pensive now and there are several brief silences during which something told me to keep quiet. Miss Herman found her a teacher, Sadie Munroe. At first she'd spent Wednesday afternoons after school learning with four other children, but she soon got to the stage of needing one-to-one tuition, so had been taught by Sadie on her own. Sadie had been a patient and nurturing mentor, one who expected, and got, commitment. She'd insisted on facing up to the challenge of taking the Grade exams – which her gifted pupil had sailed through – and playing in the County Youth Orchestra. At first this had been a terrifying experience and she'd been glad to share the bus journeys to the weekly rehearsals with the only other player from Blackbird Leys, Micky Collins, a lad who played the trumpet. The orchestra was meant to be a leveller – and indeed it was to quite an extent in that most of the children were from state schools – but she and Micky both knew that their parents could barely afford their bus fares, let alone the ponies and foreign holidays that many of the other players talked about.

I ask for more detail on what Sadie's influence had been. Another brief silence, but now I'm almost certain she will carry on. She knows the story needs finishing. I feel confident that I can reel my fish in now.

Sadie lived off the Cowley Road, in a tiny house on East Avenue, and gave her a lesson every Saturday morning. Then they'd often have a snack together before the journey back to Blackbird Leys where her mum would be home from work. The chats over a cheese sandwich helped her through her teenage years when she was inevitably growing away from her home life on the estate. She could talk to Sadie not only about her feelings about her music but also her sense of displacement and alienation from her school contemporaries. I ask her to say a bit more about this. She makes a face, and her voice hardens. 'People talk about raising aspirations but they think that everyone should aspire to what *they* think is important. If you come from a world with a different way of living, having what they call aspiration takes you away from your roots, your peers, your community, your family. I had some good friends at school, but when you practise for even an hour or two every day, more at weekends, you can't hang out down the shops, or go to the Youth Club. Your mates don't understand, they think you're a snob. I wanted to be in the gang, but I wanted to play music more, and paid the price.'

As sixth form time drew closer the subject of her future would come up. Sadie had sensed a growing loss of enthusiasm, and practice between lessons didn't seem to be happening like it used to. She knew better than to ask directly, but what eventually emerged was that at a Youth Orchestra rehearsal a few weeks earlier a group of music teachers had been chatting in the Ladies' toilets.

'Who's that little black girl in the first violins? She's really good – fabulous playing'.

'Comes from Blackbird Leys – Maggie Herman spotted her. Hopeless family – single mum, no one knows who the father is. Maggie pays for her lessons and fiddle hire.'

The 'little black girl' who overheard this stayed seething in her cubicle until they'd gone. She wasn't that little, she was 15 by now, tall and striking. She was totally mortified that Miss Herman had been deceiving her all these years about who was paying for her, furious that anyone would talk about her and her mum like that. It made her want to give up music, leave school, get a job and live a life she felt comfortable in.

I'm a bit puzzled by this – why was this discovery so shattering? There is a hint of exasperation in her voice as she explains the discomfort of feeling patronised, and that she had unknowingly incurred a personal debt. On top of that she had felt anger at having been deceived – by Sadie as well. Over the next few weeks Sadie had helped her to see that Miss Herman had been trying to protect her from just the feelings that the discovery had triggered – and that she had meant well – but it took quite a few Saturday mornings to get things back on an even keel. She didn't feel sufficiently comfortable with Miss Herman to bring up how she felt, although she knew Sadie must have told her. When they met up, which they did from time to time, things were a bit strained between them.

One Saturday Sadie suggested they go into town after the lesson to see the violins in the Ashmolean Museum – the Stradivarius known as the Messiah was the special attraction – to be followed by tea and cake in the café. They caught a number 5 bus at the James St bus stop, got off at Carfax and walked down Cornmarket Street, past Debenhams and Boswells until they got to Beaumont Street. Maybe Sadie was hoping that the grandeur of the museum and the impact of seeing a Strad that not only hadn't been played for half a century, but would probably never be played again, would produce some kind of magic. It seemed to work: 'As soon as I saw it I knew I wanted to be good enough to play a Strad.'

To be honest I find that a bit far-fetched, but realising the limits of my musical understanding I keep quiet, listening to her account of the next few years; how she redoubled her efforts on her instrument, slogged away at her academic work and got a scholarship to the Royal College of Music. She talks at some length of those times, the wrench of leaving home and living in London, how she did and didn't adjust, and how her career started and eventually took off; the travel, the role models she'd studied with, the people she met and her marriage to Thomas.

My interview had been commissioned because tonight

she was to be the star turn at a concert at the Sheldonian Theatre in Oxford, the first time she had played in her home city in over ten years. 'Will your mum be there?' I asked. Her expression darkened. 'No' she said sharply. 'She's dead and I definitely don't talk about that'. I apologise, realising that this really is a taboo subject. Mollified (I hope), she adds that she's hoping Miss Herman and Sadie Munroe will be coming – she's sent them some tickets.

Trying hard to come back to what she would talk about, I ask whether she would want any of her children to have the life she's living now, whether the distance she's travelled and the sacrifices she's made to get to the top have been worth it.

'Yes, but only just. When I'm actually playing, when I'm past the nerves and immersed in the music it's almost like succumbing to an addiction. Then at the end when I emerge from the kind of trance I get into and hear the appreciation and the cheers, and someone comes out with the flowers, I feel like looking around for who they are applauding. How can I possibly be the object of such admiration? It's weird – I sort of feel unreal, that I don't deserve it.' She pauses, looking pensive. 'But of course it's a buzz. I never stop enjoying the music, and the pleasure of playing together with an orchestra. If any of my children do it, at least they won't have their roots dragged up, like I did. They won't need to step outside the box they were born in, like I had to'.

She looks at her watch. 'Look, I'm really sorry but I'm running a bit short of time. I want to go over the road and have a look at the Messiah before tonight. Why don't you come too?' She can tell I'm a bit miffed at being cut short. 'Come on,' she says, laughing, 'I've given away a lot more than I ever have before.' I realise I've landed my fish and got enough stuff to write up. I'm flattered that she's asking me to join her, so I thank her for her time, switch off my recorder, pay the bill and we cross the road into the Ashmolean.

'Wow!' she says as we enter the newly refurbished museum. 'I heard it had been done up but this is amazing!' And indeed it is. We find the new musical instruments room and pause to look at the display which sets out how a violin is made. We agree on how interesting and illuminating that is for both of us – she who is who she is and me, a relative ignoramus. Then we look reverently at the Messiah in its glass case. To me it looks like any other violin, but she is clearly quite moved by it. 'I can't quite describe it,' she says,' but there is something so poignant about it being unplayed, a Stradivarius of all things. It's such a waste, all that potential that will never be realised.'

It slowly dawns on me what she's saying, how close she feels she came to being like the Strad in the glass box, unheard, her promise unredeemed.

That night in the Sheldonian Theatre I sit feet away from the orchestra, in a seat that she had managed to get for me behind the second violins, and listen to the first piece of music on the programme, mostly in a haze of incomprehension. If I'm honest I spend most of it writing up my interview in my head. Then she comes on, shimmering in her beautiful red silk dress, and plays her socks off.

I have only ever been to three or four classical concerts in my life, none of which particularly grabbed me, but this – Bruch's Number One Violin Concerto – is something else. I am bowled over by the virtuosity she brings to the passion and romance of the music. The applause is thunderous and prolonged, the flowers magnificent. There are shouts of

'Bravo!' as she bows and smiles with elegance and grace.

In the interval I go downstairs to the Green Room, as she'd invited me to. As I am let through the door I see her, being approached by two elderly women. I hesitate, watch her fling her arms round them both at once, laughing and – I can see – crying. I realise who they are – and that I am not part of the story.

From Here to There

NEIL HANCOX

Sam was scooping the froth from her cappuccino and I was thinking about Fulham's prospects in their next home game.

She looked at me and smiled. 'Why don't we go to Oxford next Sunday, Gil?'

First I should explain my name. Gil is short for Gilbert. Why two ordinary people, from the 1970s, should choose to call their brand new infant Gilbert is still beyond me. I never liked the name and quickly became Gil.

Since there was no match on Sunday hence, I agreed. A trip to foreign parts, as I thought of Oxford, would make a change.

'You should get your hair trimmed, wear a decent jacket and no trainers, please,' she added.

I suppose I should have been insulted by these instructions. I regard myself as scruffily elegant – real retro clothes can be very expensive. But I loved being with Sam and I was intrigued instead. I never gave it another thought, except, of course, to visit the barber and polish my shoes; Sam has that effect on me.

So that is how two people, one elegant in a summer dress, possibly with a red belt and matching shoes, if I had been observant, and the other so neatly attired that his mates would have gasped and remarked that something was up and he had better be careful, arrived at Oxford bus station at noon one Sunday. The bus driver, looking forward to a cup of coffee, the sports pages and a chat, hardly noticed them.

'It's this way,' Sam said, leading me across the bus forecourt to a busy street. I stuffed the newspaper, open at the half completed crossword, into my jacket pocket. We fought against the flow of tourists for a few minutes until we came to a junction.

Sam stopped, oriented us by turning her back to Worcester College, and pointed. 'That,' she said, 'is Beaumont Street.'

'So what,' I said, 'is Beaumont Street?'

'It's a street. It's what it says on the tin.' There was a slight acerbity in her tone.

The allusion was temporally lost on me, showing perhaps that I don't watch enough TV.

I retorted, in what I thought a suitable and rather witty manner, 'I see Beaumont Street gets you from here to there and that shows what a difference the letter t makes.'

Sam ignored my remark. 'Beaumont, beautiful mount,' she said. 'You did pass your GCSE French?' There was a questioning tone to her voice.

A cough, silence. Academically, I am more of a woodwork man but I didn't want to spoil the moment.

'See the plaque across the street.' Sam pointed with an elegant red nail. I didn't often see her with nail varnish; the thought passed, and then I heard her say, 'It commemorates the birth place of two English kings, a Richard and John.'

I had difficulty in seeing anything through the throng of people and traffic and, if I had, well history wasn't my thing either. Not that I am uneducated; I did my time at the other place, you know 'the fenland poly', and enjoyed sport, ballroom dancing and drinking while avoiding the more cerebral elements. This time I replied, 'Yes.' Any further comment was interrupted by a dishevelled youth on a ramshackle bicycle riding down the pavement clutching a pizza. A typical Oxford student, Sam assured me as I detached myself from the safety of the wall.

The tourist lecture continued. 'Further up the street, on your left is the Ashmolean Museum, on the right is the Playhouse and at the top end is the Randolph Hotel, and then across the road the Martyrs' Memorial.'

A car, driven by some testosterone-fuelled moron with a blown silencer to match, roared past and I missed our final destination; was it the hotel, which would be welcome as I was beginning to feel hungry, or to join the martyrs at the memorial, which I did not fancy. I'm not into martyrdom.

We strolled along, hand in hand, contemplating the buildings and, in my case, wondering where we would end up.

The next hazard was Gloucester Street. 'That leads to the underground car park,' Sam told me, 'which is presumably called the Gloucester Street car park, I surmised.'

The grip on my hand tightened in a way that was not entirely loving. Had I overstepped the mark in some way known only to the female psyche?

Naturally on a busy day cars were streaming in and out, so we waited at the kerbside for a gap to appear. A sudden gust of wind moulded Sam's dress to her body, emphasising every contour and crevice. My God she was desirable; I forgot hunger, puzzlement, everything, and gasped for breath. How I wanted her. The breeze vanished and it was all a memory.

'Are you alright Gil?' Sam asked as I stared with unfocused eyes into space, my mouth slightly open.

I hauled my attention back to the present. 'Fine.'

The traffic slowed for a moment and we hurried across the side street and walked on towards the Playhouse. As we passed the entrance a door was pushed open and an agitated youth dashed out and stopped us. 'Are you two Romeo and Juliet?' he gulped. He looked at us again, 'No you are too old. Sorry.'

Sam didn't seem to mind but I was annoyed. I wanted to grab him; I tried to think of some Shakespearean character, Julius Caesar maybe, and say that a lout like him would never make a prince and if he didn't watch out he'd feel the tip of my sword. Too late, by then a rucksack, that curse of the crowded bus, train or pavement, pushed me off balance, while a twin buggy nearly took out my legs. Bloody people. This was worse than playing football, I muttered, while massaging a shin.

Sanctuary was at hand, the entrance to the Randolph Hotel. Sam pulled me in, kissed me quickly but hard, took the paper out of my pocket and dumped it and led me through towards the bar. What was she playing at? Why the sudden public display of affection? Anyway things were looking up; I could do with a pint. I checked that I had my cards with me; I would be the perfect escort and pay for the drinks.

'Hi there,' she shouted.

I looked. There were four people waiting at the far end of the bar; a tall man and a short, let's face it, dumpy woman, obviously a couple of long standing and, to one side, a solid bloke about my age with an equally solid woman, who looked as though they were present in response to a three-line whip. Sam rushed over and exchanged kisses and hugs, while I hung back assessing the ales on offer.

She pulled me over. 'And this is Gil,' she said, as though I was exhibit number one. And then, 'Mum and Dad and my brother and his partner,' she indicated the four people. 'I've told them all about you,' she added. Handshakes, yes, kisses, no. I smiled of course and said how pleased I was to meet them. Things began to slot into place: the sudden suggestion of a trip to Oxford, the smart appearance. I was up to meet the family, to be inspected. My God had her biological alarm clock suddenly rung? Would I be taken aside by Dad and asked the date of the wedding?

Sam and I had met at a theme party. That was six or seven months ago. I'm not good at anticipation. For me life is full of surprises and this was certainly one; it's probably a male thing.

'Let's go through to lunch,' Mum said, taking both my arm and control of the proceedings. 'And do call us Mum and Dad.'

I swallowed; my legs were going again; fortunately the round table crowded with glasses and cutlery was nearby. The parents and Sam sat on one arc while I was sandwiched between brother and partner opposite. It reminded me of a military disciplinary hearing with the prisoner's friend on one side and the guard on the other.

I briefly reviewed my table manners: start at the outside with the cutlery and work inwards, and don't eat peas with your knife. The waiter, I was sure, would know which glass to fill. That would help.

The inquisition started immediately if not subtly.

'You don't live in Oxford, do you Gil? Where were you at university? Sam tells me you're an entrepreneur.'

You get the idea; Torquemada came to mind or was he a central defender for Real Madrid? I nearly asked if Mum had been a specialist interrogator with MI5; unsure of her sense of humour, my nerve failed. Short of giving a tissue sample for a detailed DNA analysis she had my life and times laid bare by the arrival of cheese and biscuits.

I hadn't been offered a cigarette beforehand, which I recalled was the case in wartime spy films. Fortunately the wine was excellent, a claret I learnt from the bottle, and this helped me relax. The waiter refilled my glass so frequently that I began to wonder if there was a hole in the bottom. That and a total absence of peas from the menu saw me through the ordeal. I was now used to the darting birdlike questions and had mastered the art of ducking and weaving long enough to give myself time to concoct plausible answers.

There was one moment of panic, that strikes us all occasionally, even the most stout- hearted. Sam was smiling serenely, almost glowing. I suddenly wondered – she wasn't, she couldn't be, could she? I glanced around surreptitiously looking for the shotgun.

Mum must have noticed my discomfort. 'It's a bit hot in here,' she said. 'Take your jacket off if you want, Gil.'

By now I had control of my emotions again. 'I'm OK, really; I'd better take a little water with the wine,' I joked.

Brother had exquisite table manners; every time his phone rang he excused himself.' It was,' his partner observed in one of her rare excursions into the spoken word, 'surprising that he ate anything,' or was so weighty, in body if not mind, I thought.

If she was to be Mum, her husband might as well complete the happy family by being Dad, and Dad was lugubrious. I was uncertain what the word meant but instinctively knew it applied to the old man; he had hollow and lined cheeks, spare tanned wrists and hands, a mop of white hair well secured to his head, and a body encased in well-worn tweed which hung off his frame. Conversationally he agreed or kept his silence. To complete the tableau he skilfully intercepted the eventual bill, proffered a card and tapped in the appropriate digits. With thanks all round, and relief on my part, we left the table for coffee and sweetmeats in the lounge.

The chairs were comfortable and the combination of food and drink caused a certain degree of drowsiness. Conversation was desultory – traffic, house prices – we even ventured onto the fortunes of Oxford United, though quickly left them. As four o'clock approached it was time for parting. Kisses all round from Sam, two quick pecks on two proffered cheeks and handshakes from me.

We stepped into the outside world and I inhaled deeply of fresh air and fumes; ah what relief, I thought, before I began to cough violently.

Sam patted me on the back. 'Now,' she said, 'we must go from there to here.'

I was fighting shock, fatigue and alcohol, and failed to interpret her remark at first. By the time words had clicked into place, Sam was pulling me gently along, back down her faithful street.

'That was fun,' she said, 'Mum and Dad really liked you.'

I knew I should reply with a suitable comment but a mental paralysis was creeping up on me, mesmerising me and constraining my ability to respond; it was pleasant.

Perhaps this was how fundamentalists and fanatics felt; decisions made for them, limbs moved automatically as though their direction was preordained.

I did have a theory, however. Sam was an orphan and she had hired the family I had just met to assess me objectively and also convince me of her normal background. The report was probably being finalised at this moment to appear shortly on her mobile.

'Careful!' Sam's shout broke the spell, as she hauled me out of the path of an oncoming car. It was, I realised in a detached way, a top of the market BMW; if you were going to be run down choose a good quality assassin. Sam looked concerned, I smiled and kissed her. And the driver swore.

'Sorry, love,' I said, 'I must concentrate.'

I never did air my theory.

The Henbury Plastics Convention

JENNY BURRAGE

Peter Richard Ford was hopping mad. He stared gloomily through the windscreen wipers, mesmerised by the monotonous action of the blades. Everything annoyed him. He was, as Sheila would have put it, in one of his black moods.

He hated Monday mornings and this one was worse than usual. Log jams, road rage, hooting, and the fucking commercials on Classic FM peppering his beloved Bach. No he didn't want a stair lift thank you very much. He was only forty nine for Christ's sake!

He viciously punched one of the buttons to his left and the window hummed down obligingly. Air, that's what he needed. A gulp of traffic-laden polluted air. As the car came to a standstill for the umpteenth time, he looked at himself in the mirror. James Bond stared back at him. Everyone told him he looked just like Daniel Craig. He had to admit it was true. What a handsome chap he was. He almost smiled to himself.

He knew they shouldn't have had the neighbours in last night. That had been a mistake on a Sunday evening, especially the night before the mega important annual convention in Oxford's famous Randolph Hotel, awaiting him at the end of a two-hour drive.

'We'd better be going,' the so-called friends had offered

unconvincingly. The time then was ten thirty and he'd heard that one before and of course, true to form, they'd finally stumbled off at around one. They were all the worse for drink, he more than the others.

He'd allotted that evening to check over the work he'd been preparing for the last week. And now here he was crawling along the M40 with an empty mind and a thick head. The accident a couple of miles back hadn't helped. He was going to be late. It was all Sheila's fault. She had done the inviting without a word to him.

'Our turn, dear,' she'd said.

The empty wine bottles had faced him accusingly, lined up across the kitchen work top like a firing squad as he'd entered the kitchen that morning. Carrying a tatty looking briefcase in his hand and with his tie at half mast, he gave Sheila the customary peck on the cheek. After twenty-five years what more did she expect?

She was clearing up the debris of the night before and was still wearing her woolly red dressing gown and brown furry slippers.

'See you tomorrow then.' She hardly looked up.

'Yes.'

'Good luck, dear.' He had felt like throttling her.

He'd slammed the door behind him, cross with himself, cross with her, cross with the whole world.

Peter Richard Ford parked his car in Gloucester Green car park for its overnight stay. After several years attending the convention, he knew the routine. He hurried down Beaumont Street and entered the Randolph Hotel, through its huge black doors with shiny brass handles. Behind a small glass partition next to reception were some articles for sale. One was a book by Colin Dexter. The title seemed to cruelly loom out at him: The Remorseful Day. He was feeling that his day was going to end just like that title and it hadn't even started yet.

This was his fifth convention. It was a time when sales figures were revealed, awards given out, promotions considered, and redundancies inevitable. It was, to put it bluntly, payment by result. He'd been lucky so far, considering the precarious nature of a salesman's job. It was all routine by now, but at the same time there was always a threat and the past year had not been good.

His bleary eyes squinted at a small board in the foyer announcing the list of hotel activities for that day.

'Hotel Macdonald Randolph welcomes its visitors,' he read sullenly, and then his glance alighted on the dreaded oh so familiar directions:

HENBURY PLASTICS
ANNUAL SALES CONVENTION TODAY
THE BALLROOM
11am

He looked at his watch. Oh fucking hell, 11.45. They would be breaking for lunch soon. His heart skipped a beat.

His untimely entrance would surely be noticed and noted down by the hierarchy as a blot on the proverbial copy book. There wasn't time to check in. He only had his briefcase anyway, always shoved a clean shirt and toothbrush in with his presentation stuff. He nodded at the woman behind the reception desk and mumbled something incoherent about being late. She smiled sympathetically at him as he headed for the dreaded conference room.

Unfortunately for him there was only one vacant place amongst the chairs which had been laid out, and naturally it was on the end of the front row.

Horror of horrors, Theodore E. Green Senior, the American president of the company, was holding forth as Peter Richard Ford sidled into the ballroom. There seemed to him a deathly silence as he settled himself down, almost cringing under the speaker's gaze. A mass of faces had turned towards him as he entered.

His briefcase, which he placed gingerly on the floor, seemed to make a thud which reverberated round the room.

'And finally,' drawled Mr Speaker 'I want you all to know that I'm proud of you at Henbury Plastics and I want you to always remember our three P's when you are selling our products around the UK. Now come on you guys, let's hear it one more time for Henbury Plastics.'

He cupped his hand round his ear as if expecting the assembled company to respond, which of course they did, like robots. The pin-striped suited area managers and the worthy salesmen and women obediently chanted with one voice:

'Perspicacity, Power and Punctuality!'

On the last word the speaker cast an evil sidelong glance at the poor unfortunate latecomer and it was just as well that the loud applause drowned the patriotic ringing tones of the national anthem on his mobile phone. Who the hell would phone him at this time? He hoped it wasn't Sheila. He would have words with her if it was.

It wasn't until he'd located the phone in the depths of the crap that composed the interior of the briefcase and switched it off that he noticed the woman sitting beside him. His heart once again missed a beat but for a different reason this time.

She was indeed nothing more nor less than an angel. That had to be her name. He christened her silently. Angel. He mouthed the words to himself. A lovely sound. Her long blonde hair swirled over the collar of her jacket. Her sparkling white teeth neatly displayed beneath ruby lips smiled at him. Her elegant black trouser suit showed off a perfectly proportioned body.

'Hard luck,' she whispered. 'Late night?'

He nodded, spellbound, lost for words. How did she know? She understood his situation perfectly. She must be a kindred spirit. Her words soothed him instantly and he gazed at her longingly. Next minute she had gathered up her papers and vanished into the crowd who were heading off for lunch.

He was absolutely dumbfounded! Was it possible to fall for someone in an instant? Surely not. He was happily married or so he thought. Twenty-five years, near enough. Bit of a rut admittedly but he'd never strayed from his wife. An image of Sheila as he had left her that morning, in the familiar red dressing gown, wafted before his eyes.

His thoughts moved back to Angel. Their eyes had met across a crowded room. That old chestnut went through his mind. He'd heard it often enough but this time Angel had been sitting on the next seat to him and their eyes had met sideways. Different contact point, but still powerful.

He had noticed sadly she was wearing a wedding ring but

then so was he for that matter. What on earth was up with him thinking stupid thoughts like a teenager?

He suddenly realised he was sitting dreaming in the conference room alone, although not quite alone. He felt a tap on his shoulder and the large bulky presence of his boss loomed in front of his bleary lovesick eyes. He was brought back to horrible reality.

'Ford!' it boomed, 'I'm glad I caught you. Didn't look good for us you coming in late like that. Did us no good at all.'

'Sorry. The traffic on the M40 was a pig.'

'I come that route as you well know, Ford, but I set off promptly at six am and I had no trouble getting here, no trouble at all.'

'Sorry.'

It was all Peter Richard Ford could think of to say. As his immediate area manager, he considered Frank Goddard a nasty piece of work. He was someone who gloated over obvious faults in his underlings. It gave him an opportunity to give them a right old ticking off and put himself on a pedestal.

He looked at Goddard standing there, red faced and towering over him.

'You missed my contribution this morning, Ford, and although I say it myself, I think our president was impressed. Could be a place on the Board for me. My feeling was he recognised talent right away. He approached me immediately afterwards. Came up to me like lightning! Banged on the table. I could almost see the steam coming out of his ears. Passionate response I'd say. He must have been moved by what he heard.

'He told me he'd never heard the like before and he

immediately cancelled my trip to speak at our New York Company Shareholders' Meeting.

'I guess he realised I was needed here to keep my finger on the pulse of things. Pity you missed my words of wisdom, Ford. Never mind, I've got a copy of my notes for you to read. I'd welcome your written comments on it first thing tomorrow.'

The lecturer paused for a moment, consulting the programme in his chubby hand. His eyes narrowed and he raised his bushy eyebrows.

'I hope you've got your presentation ready for this afternoon, Ford, sales figures and forecast profits for 2016/17 in our neck of the woods. Show him what we're made of, eh?'

'Yes indeed,' lied his sales rep. He followed his fat boss into lunch in a daze, not even remembering to check in.For Peter Richard Ford, it is probably better that we draw a veil over most of the afternoon's events. After lunch, he still felt headachy and drowsy as the hangover drifted on like a storm cloud. He'd spent most of the lunch break, when he'd managed to escape from Frank Goddard, in the conference room, cobbling together some facts and figures for his matinee performance and checking out the viewing equipment for his PowerPoint demonstration. Some slides would show a graph with falling sale results. He would eliminate those.

What was worse was that when it came to his presentation, the delectable Angel was sitting in the very same place on the front row, this time under his very nose. It was disconcerting to say the least.

He waffled his way through his notes with the

accompanying screen presentation, trying to disguise the fact that Henbury Plastics, in his area at least, had made an overall loss.

To the audience most of what he said was incomprehensible, but like the gullible people in the story of The Emperor's New Clothes, they had no desire to show their ignorance.

Theodore E. Green on the other hand stared darkly at him as he rabbited on. The president studied the programme and made a mental note to confront this pathetically unprepared salesman with an ultimatum, not to mention his equally incompetent area manager, one F. Goddard. Heads would roll at their area meeting the following week and new appointments be made.

The rest of the shuffling and yawning audience, unaware of the impending doom for Mr P.R. Ford, were relieved but somewhat surprised to hear his closing words.

'I want to thank you all for listening to me this afternoon. You have all been so… er… so… beautiful. His eyes were focusing on the alluring Angel and the tremor in his voice brought a small ripple of polite applause from the delegates.

At ten o'clock precisely, Peter Richard Ford could no longer keep his eyes open. He'd spent the last hour in The Randolph's famous Morse bar as he listened to the drone of Frank Goddard's foghorn of a voice. He had been collared by him at dinner and hadn't been able to escape. There was no sign of the fair Angel in the restaurant but at least he had eaten. Now he was stuck with his objectionable boss.

He felt like punching him in the middle of his huge paunch which hung over his trousers in a most boastful manner. Peter Richard Ford had hardly spoken a word in all that time, only nodded and shaken his head occasionally. He hoped the gorgeous Angel would come into the bar but there was no sign of her.

'I'm bushed,' he told Frank eventually.

He was past caring whether or not he offended him by retiring early. In any case he had a nasty feeling his job would be on the line anyway after his abysmal performance today. And after hearing the president's response to Frank's presentation, he thought he might be up for dismissal as well. What was worse, they would all have to suffer the final words from the President the following morning. He wished he could drive home right now but he was under close supervision from his boss.

The fat man looked disdainfully at him as if he were a wimp, unable to stand the pace.

He finally collected his room key card and checked in to room number 36 on the first floor. He hadn't understood why the chap on the reception desk had told him that it was a duplicate key but he was too weary to ask why. He didn't really care. All he wanted to do was get his head down.

The first thing he noticed as he entered room number 36 was that there was a tray with the remains of a meal lying on the small table in the window.

The second thing was the heap of clothes on the floor; looked like black lacy underwear no less.

The third thing was a musky rose smell filling number 36.

The fourth and most incredible to him was a light coming from the en suite and the sound of someone moving about in there.

Peter Richard Ford, being a man of action, knocked

tentatively on the bathroom door.

'Hello,' he called. 'Who is that in my bathroom?' Just somehow he knew what was going to happen next. Call it a premonition if you like. The door opened.

Into the room stepped the wondrous Angel wrapped only in a fluffy white towel bearing the Randolph logo, her shapely legs revealed to him for the first time.

She didn't scream as one might have expected. Suddenly it all dawned on him. She had obviously fallen for him as he had for her and planned this wonderful seduction. She had found out his room number and posed as his girlfriend. Hence the duplicate key. He no longer felt tired. In fact there was a stirring in his lower body the like of which he hadn't felt for a long, long time. Fate was on his side for the first time today.

'Hello again. What are you doing in my room?' she asked him.

'I could ask you the same question,' he replied, puzzled that she was reacting like this. She must have known it was his. What was going on?

'Look this is ridiculous,' she said. 'Reception must have made a mistake. I'll phone down. By the way, I'm Sara Ford.' She held out her hand to him.

'Peter Richard Ford.' He returned her handshake.

Suddenly it all clicked into place. They both twigged what had happened at the same moment.

'Mr and Mrs Ford,' they almost shouted in unison.

'Good old Henbury central administration department,' she smiled. 'They assumed we were husband and wife.'

They looked at each other and then they started laughing. It was all so ludicrous. Their laughter got louder and louder.

Tears were streaming down his face. Sara collapsed onto the bed, totally helpless, her sides aching as if she'd been relentlessly tickled.

'You really are an angel.' He couldn't help telling her. He wanted to savour the moment. For what seemed like an eternity they both said nothing. He gazed at her, unable to move.

'You're really sweet, Peter Richard Ford.'

There was a silence. He wanted to kiss her but he didn't dare.

She stood up and put her arms around him, letting the towel drop to the floor. He gasped.

'Well Mr Ford,' she whispered in his ear, 'if they really believe we are Mr and Mrs, we might as well make the most of it.'

'Mrs Ford, you are absolutely right,' he murmured softly, as instinctively they moved towards the bed.

'What the eye doesn't see, Mrs Ford … Mmm?'

'My sentiments exactly, Mr Ford.'

Peter Richard Ford now was certain he had died and gone to heaven. And the rest as they say is history.

Sheila Ford had greeted her husband somewhat coldly on his return from the conference. After all, he never went away for the night without phoning her. She had waited till the small hours hoping for a call. But it never came. He looked haggard and much more tired than usual after previous conventions, she thought. He must have been stressed. He was obviously worn out after what had gone on.

She suddenly felt guilty that she'd been so cool with him and promised herself she'd cook his favourite boeuf en croute that very evening. It was rather fiddly to prepare but he was worth it. She also decided to miss the WI meeting that evening. She didn't want to leave him on his own.

So later on, over the special supper she had so lovingly cooked, she decided to ask him about his trip. He seemed so remote and his mind far away. He hadn't even commented on the meal or the fact she was wearing her new sparkly jumper.

'How did it go then, Peter?'

'How did what go?' He wasn't really listening and he didn't want to communicate with her anyway. This whole meal was a bore. He wanted Angel back in his arms.

'You know, the Henbury Plastics do, of course?'

He thought about this for a while and then he started shouting.

'There's nothing I want to talk about right now, Sheila. What do you want to hear? If you must know I was bloody late arriving. I made a cock-up of my presentation. I'll probably lose my job. Goddard was his usual swinish self. He might get the push as well. The President was a jerk. Forget it.'

'I'm sure things won't be as bad as that, dear.' Sheila brought in the apple crumble, another special treat. They didn't usually have a pudding.

At that moment Peter Richard Ford calmed down and the change of mood had nothing to do with the crumble. He smiled a secret smile, mulling over last night with Sara, his ravishing Angel. He could remember running his fingers over every inch of her exquisite body in Room 36.

'I can't possibly tell you all the ins and outs,' he said, still grinning to himself.

Host your next conference in Oxford and benefit from the services and amenities at the Macdonald Randolph Hotel. The beautiful city of Oxford is the ideal venue for your next conference, boasting a unique urban setting surrounded by English countryside. From the Randolph Hotel website.

Alistair's Evening Out

GEOFF BREMBLE

It was 5.00 pm when Alistair, aged 13, arrived at school to be the first to board the coach that was taking a school party for a special one-off guided tour of the Ashmolean Museum. His mother, the school's headmistress, had dropped him off and seated him in the front seat next to Mr Brown, the teacher in charge of the visit. Alistair was an awkward-looking boy, with thin arms and legs attached to a long skinny torso. He had only been at the school a few days and had yet to break down the natural suspicions towards a new boy, particularly one whose parent was in a position of total power.

As the coach sped towards its destination Alistair, alone and friendless, made up his mind to be the last one to get off. On arrival he didn't move until all the other children had alighted, after which he reluctantly stepped down onto the pavement. He remained there, hidden from view, pondering what to do next. The giant doors of the Ashmolean suddenly opened and within minutes all the children had disappeared inside. The doors closed leaving Alistair alone on the street, he hesitated for a minute or two before reasoning that he had no choice. He walked up the steps, crossed the terrace and as he did so the doors reopened. He stepped inside to an eerie silence and, with no other children in sight, the doors closed silently behind him. He stood for a minute allowing his eyes to adjust to the dim light of the entrance.

'What do I do now?' he murmured to himself while glancing at his watch, which read 6.00 pm exactly.

He walked through the revolving door into the foyer and heard sounds coming from a gallery to his left. He was unable to hear what was being said so took a step inside to find three men and one woman seated in a circle. Two of the men wore no clothes while the woman and the other man were partially clothed in flowing robes. One of the men was stroking a lion that lay across his lap. But what was more disconcerting was that all, including the lion, had gleaming white skin, hair and robes and no other colouring. The most imposing of the men, albeit minus his right hand, was seated on a throne. It was he who spoke.

'Come in young man, we weren't expecting you, but as you are now here may I introduce myself and my companions. I am Jupiter, the Roman God of sky and thunder, and King of all the Gods.'

He then swept his good arm round towards those seated next to him.

'First on my left is Heracles, God of heroes and champion of the Olympic order. The lion on his lap is named Nemean, and next to him is Dionysus, God of grapes and all pleasures. Last but not least is their sister Aphrodite, Goddess of love and beauty. Unfortunately she has lost her head, an arm and a hand thanks to clumsy handling on her journey from ancient Greece.'

He paused and Aphrodite took the opportunity to butt in.

'We're not actual Gods but have been carved out of marble

and brought here for the education of you young people,' she explained, 'and Heracles is also called Hercules, but if you want to know why you'll have to find that out for yourself.'

Alistair stared at the group in disbelief. But it was Aphrodite's ability to speak that disturbed him most, her voice seeming to come from a position where her mouth would have been had she had a head. It was then that he saw, further down the gallery, what appeared to be fully clothed beings. They were all about seven feet tall and talking animatedly to each other in languages he could not comprehend.

'Don't worry about them,' Jupiter assured Alistair, 'they're speaking in a mixture of ancient tongues and will cause you no harm.'

Alistair suddenly found his voice and, averting his gaze from the naked torsos, he introduced himself.

'My name is Alistair and I wonder if you can help me. I've just arrived at the Museum with a school party but they seem to have disappeared.'

'They certainly have,' Jupiter began with a laugh. 'They all charged through here in a rush wanting to get to what they deem to be the more interesting sights. But I'm afraid you're too late to catch up with them and, being alone, you are now in deep trouble.'

'But I don't want to cause any trouble, can't I just go back and wait at the entrance for them to return?' Alistair responded.

'Sorry, no, the doors you came in by can't be opened from this side without you having been through the Museum and as you make your way there will be beings who might want to harm you.' He paused, gathering his thoughts as to what to say next.

'Oh get on with it,' chimed in Heracles, followed by an aside to Alistair, 'you'll have by now realised that our Jupiter loves the sound of his own voice. What he's trying to say is that in order to escape you have to get round to the exit within a certain time. However it is unfortunate for you that our time system is different from yours. We mark ours out by that timer on the table; it holds 10,000 grains of sand which flow from the top to the bottom, flowing faster as the number of grains in the top become fewer. It started timing you as soon as you stepped into the gallery, and as it stands now you have 7840 grains of time left. Now, I'll leave Jupiter to tell you what the implications are if you don't make it in time.'

As Jupiter responded Alistair took a quick glance at his watch – it still read 6.00 pm.

'Thank you Heracles for such an erudite explanation. It's most important that he knows the situation he's in. Now where was I? Oh yes, when we know visitors are coming to gaze at us we take up our exhibition positions and go into what can only be described as a catatonic state. This means we go into our natural state, which for us is marble. However, when we are sure that nobody is here we relax into how we are now. Unfortunately security has let us down today, allowing you to find us in this state. The problem we have is that if your world gets to know that we have two states of being we would be probed and jabbed by who knows how many learned scientists. They would want to know how it is that this dual way of life can exist. So, in order to protect our secret, when a Loner finds us as we are now some of our brethren take it upon themselves to prevent them leaving the

Museum. If I remember correctly, we've had six such Loners since the Ashmolean opened its doors and none escaped.'

'What do you mean none escaped? Where are they now?' interrupted an increasingly anxious 13 year old.

'I'm just coming to that,' was Jupiter's response. 'If any of those of us who are inclined to prevent you leaving touch your skin, or even a piece of your clothing, you will instantaneously be turned to stone. You would then be transported into storage and hidden amongst the plethora of exhibits that are in the Museum's vaults. You would never be seen or heard of again. And what's more your fate will be the same if you are still in the Museum when your time runs out.'

'That's not fair! I wasn't looking to find you, I didn't even know that you existed before I got here,' responded a now angry Alistair who was becoming aware of the dangerous situation he was in.

'Calm down, we'll help you escape. We realise that nobody would believe you at all if you tried to explain what you had seen, but however hard we try we can never convince some of our other brethren to believe that. I'm afraid to say that a lack of education in their former life is probably the cause.'

Alistair listened to all this, his mouth and eyes wide open, unable to take it all in except to know that he had to get to the Museum exit fast.

'But who are these people?' demanded Alistair.

'That you will be told on the way. First of all I will direct you to Captain T. E. Lawrence – author, archaeologist, military officer, diplomat and friend of the Arab nation – who resides in the basement. He will help you get round the first obstacle and will direct you on to a Buddha who, in turn, will instruct you as to how to proceed, and so on until hopefully you are able to escape. During your journey you will be kept informed as to how many grains of time you have left. Are you ready to face what lies ahead?'

'Yes, I think so,' Alistair responded, not too convincingly. Jupiter put his good arm round Alistair's shoulder and pointed with his stump towards the end of the room they were in.

'See down there? Well, you turn into the first gallery on the right and carry on until you see a set of stairs. Nemean will guide you down,' he said, pointing to the lion, 'and Captain Lawrence will be waiting at the bottom. Now, off you go, and I see that you've only got 7030 grains of time left so do not delay.'

Aphrodite took the opportunity to chime in again.

'What he hasn't told you is that you will also have to go past my father, the great God Zeus. He doesn't like intruders, least of all Loners. But don't worry about him, he spends most of his time admiring his body or showing off how far he can throw his javelins. He used to hurl thunderbolts but it was decided that javelins were less dangerous.'

'I was going to explain that before you interrupted,' grumbled Jupiter as, next to him, Heracles whispered instructions for Nemean to go to Alistair's side.

'Climb onto my back and hold tight,' the lion growled, after which Alistair grabbed his mane and leapt on. The pair then moved through the crowd of chattering beings, all too intent on their own business to notice them. They turned to the right as instructed and sped safely past Zeus who was taking a rest from hurling his javelins. When they reached the stairs the lion knelt on his front paws.

'You'll have to walk down. I'd carry you, only you'd be likely to fall off. You'll find Captain Lawrence waiting at the bottom but don't worry, I'll be right behind you,' he paused before adding,' and, just so you know, you have just 6130 grains left.'

Alistair moved to the top of the stairs and looked down. He descended the stairway in no time at all and found a figure, whose featureless face exhibited no nose, no mouth, no ears nor eyes. It was dressed in a flowing white robe of silk embroidered with gold and silver thread while its head was covered by a purple headdress, held there by a silk rope decorated with gold thread. Then, to Alistair's surprise, the figure began to speak.

'Welcome, I believe you are looking to escape this Museum. I am Captain Thomas Edward Lawrence, more famously known as Lawrence of Arabia.'

'Yes sir, I've heard about you and I've been told that you're going to help me get to a Buddha.'

'That is indeed true, but you have chosen just the wrong day to visit us. In the next gallery there is a Trojan priest named Laocoön and his two sons Antiphantes and Thymbraeus. They are fighting two flesh-eating snakes, and these are the first of those who, if they touch you, will cause you to meet the fate as described to you by Jupiter. Laocoön and his sons are normally in another part of the Museum, but every now and then they come into the Atrium to put on a show of wrestling for the entertainment of Museum inmates. Unfortunately today is one of those days.'

Alistair poked his head round the corner to see the father and sons, the latter appearing to be only a few years older than himself. Each boy was holding the head of a snake, their sharp, snapping fangs only inches from their faces. The monsters were wrapped around the torso, arms and legs of all three combatants in an attempt to bring them crashing to the ground.

Alistair pulled back and Captain Lawrence outlined his plan.

'We have to go through the next gallery to get to the Atrium without being seen. You then have to go round the back of it in order to get to the bottom of those stairs opposite. When you get there, Nemean will carry you up three flights of stairs where, at the top, you'll find the Buddha waiting. It will be very dark passing through the gallery but fortunately I have a lantern to guide us. It has an interesting pedigree being the one that Guy Fawkes used to light his way through the Parliament cellars when he and others attempted to assassinate King James I and his Parliament in 1605.'

'But won't the snakes follow us?'

'No, they are confined to the basement floor of the Museum so once you get past the first set of stairs you'll be safe and, of course, being carried by Nemean you'll have the advantage of speed.'

Captain Lawrence then turned to Nemean.

'I'm not sure that I can hold them on my own. I think that we should call on the Arm to assist us; after all he has helped in the past and we don't want to be remembered as the ones who lost this young man. I could use my Khanjar, but its blade is so sharp that it might cut into the snakes and I don't want to do that.'

'I agree the Arm is a good idea and that the Khanjar is not an option. What about those Javanese daggers or maybe the

American Tamahacks?'

'I don't think the Tamahacks would help as I'm sure that the Arm couldn't get one of those ball-headed clubs off the ground. I'll use the daggers, they're light and manoeuvrable and will be perfect for the job.'

'That's settled then. You carry on round to the Atrium while I go and fetch the Arm.'

Nemean then returned to the bottom of the stairs where he saw that the Arm was already up and about. He went over, plucked it out of the air and, gently holding it in his mouth, took it to the meeting point. Once there he released it and, to Alistair's amazement, a severed arm floated over to Captain Lawrence and shook his hand. Captain Lawrence then explained:

'In the Museum we have a number of spirits, benevolent ones who are only too pleased to help Loners escape and malevolent ones who are the complete opposite. They're not really bad, it's just that they worry about Loners who, if they get out, might expose our lifestyle. The Arm is made of bronze and is over 2300 years old, and it holds one of our benevolent spirits. We're not sure where it came from but presumably the rest of its body can be found in another museum somewhere else in the world. When we have the snakes under control, Nemean will be able to get to the stairway and carry you on up to the Buddha.'

He passed one of the daggers to the Arm and waited for when the heads of both of the snakes were turned away from where they were standing. It seemed like ages: first one and then the other was pulled into the right position but not both at the same time until finally,

'Hang on, we're off. Get ready to move.' Captain Lawrence

leapt into the open space with the Arm floating next to him. They had only moved a few yards before the snakes realised that a Loner was trying to pass through. They broke away from their fight and slithered towards the intruders. Laocoön and the boys tried to stop them, throwing themselves forward and grabbing at them in desperation. Captain Lawrence and the Arm stayed close, working together to block the snakes' way forward, but things began to look desperate. It seemed as if they might not succeed. It was then that the Arm caused the snakes to hesitate by swooping down to ground level and threatening them with his dagger. This hesitation allowed Nemean to seize his opportunity and, with Alistair hanging precariously on his back, he launched himself forward and raced towards the stairs. As they turned to go up, Nemean stumbled which slowed him down, almost dislodging Alistair. The lion felt the hot breath of the two snakes on his hind legs but, with a mighty effort, he was able to launch himself forward and out of reach.

At the top of this first set of stairs Nemean paused, allowing Alistair to wave his thanks to Captain Lawrence and the Arm before he and Nemean travelled on upwards.

They found the Buddha waiting for them at the top of the stairs. He was a tall man dressed in flowing robes and holding in his right hand a staff, with metal rings hanging freely in a half ring at its top. His face exuded calm, while in the middle of his forehead was a third eye, and his large, closely shaven head had two elongated ears. He smiled benignly at Alistair and spoke.

'Welcome, I am the Bodhisattva Jizo, protector of travellers, women and children. I trust your little skirmish hasn't caused you to worry about what lies ahead. As there are only 5140 grains left there's no time to lose. Are you ready to go on?'

'Yes, I think so.'

'Then follow me,' instructed Jizo. 'We turn immediately left and proceed to where, round a corner, we will find a Samurai seated on his throne. I want you to look into his eyes and then at what he has on his head-dress, but make sure you're not seen.'

The two of them moved forward to allow Alistair to take a quick look.

'But he has no eyes, it's just a blank space,' said a puzzled Alistair.

'Correct, that is because he is not a he, he is just a Samurai suit of armour. There is no Samurai inside but there is a spirit force, and an angry one at that.'

'Does that mean it won't let me get past?'

'It does, but remember, I asked you to look at what was on his head-dress. Did you see anything?'

'Well yes, I think it's a dog of some sort.'

'No, it's a lion; that is where the malevolent spirit lives and that is what you have to guard against. If you were to walk up and admire the robes the lion would leap onto you and turn you into stone.'

Alistair took another quick look.

'But can't I just go round the back of him?'

'No, he has eyes like a hawk and moves with the speed of light. As soon as you turn that corner he'll be down on the ground and racing towards you.'

'So what can I do, how can I get past him?'

'Nemean will go in before you and engage him in combat. At the right moment, when he has him under control, you must go in round the back of the Samurai suit and then get back to the corridor. Once there, turn right and around the corner you'll see a seated Bodhisattva. Her name is Guanyin; get to her as quickly as you can, touch her and you'll be safe – the Samurai lion will have to retreat. You must then carry on along the corridor to the end and take the stairway down.'

'I understand but what will happen to Nemean?'

'He can't go with you and will have to retrace his steps back to where you first met him. Now, one other thing: time is running out so don't let Guanyin delay you. She's a terrible talker and will keep you as long as she can, eating up your time, and so, in a sense, she is also a danger to you but without meaning to be.'

'Thank you for that advice. Now can we get started, you're using up my time,' responded Alistair with a quick glance at his watch, which still read 6.00 pm.

Nemean stepped out into the gallery. The Samurai lion looked across at the intruder and gave a warning roar, sending chills down Alistair's spine. Nemean advanced slowly; the Samurai lion roared again and leapt down onto the ground, making a quick movement towards him. Then in a flurry of fierce activity too quick for the eye to see the two lions came together and, within seconds, Nemean had the Samurai lion trapped on the ground.

'Quick, now run! You've only got 4105 grains left,' ordered Jizo. Alistair moved out and sprinted behind the Samurai suit, at which he heard another mighty roar and the voice of Jizo:

'Faster, faster, he can't hold him much longer!'

Alistair was still in danger; he turned into the corridor

and round the corner where he found the Buddha sitting impassively in her chair. Then came a scream from behind:

'Dive, dive for her feet – grab them!'

Alistair hurled himself headlong towards Guanyin and clutched her feet. He looked over his shoulder and saw that the Samurai lion had stopped inches from him. Its roar was one of anger and disappointment at its failure to capture its prey. Alistair didn't move while Guanyin spoke quietly to the lion. It gave one last roar and retreated back to its position on the Samurai's head-dress.

Guanyin then spoke to him: 'You may stand up, young man, you are now safe in my hands. I'm Guanyin and I am an East Asian spiritual figure of mercy and compassion as venerated by Mahayana Buddhists. Guanyin is short for Guanshiyin, which means *"Perceiving the cries of the World"*, and when adherents depart from this world I place them in the heart of a Lotus, and send them to the Western pure land of Sukhavati.'

Guanyin was speaking in a voice so soft and gentle that he felt he could sacrifice everything forever just to hear that voice speaking to him and to him alone.

From behind Alistair heard the distant voice of Jizo shouting, 'Go, go!' He shook his head and sat up, but the Buddha carried on talking, unperturbed by the shouts from Jizo and oblivious to Alistair's need for a speedy exit. He was tempted to listen to just a few more words; it was then that she paused and it was this silence that jolted him into action. He got to his feet and, without thanking her, he left and sprinted along the corridor to the next stairway. He reached the top to be confronted by a wall on which there were 16 heads, arguing as to who had made the most significant contribution to the world. As Alistair arrived, they stopped rowing amongst themselves and turned their attention to him.

'How long has he got left?' a voice shouted.

'3025 grains,' shouted one.

'No, 2700,' roared another and then all of them shouted at him in unison.

'You've only got 2260 grains left and you'd better get going or it'll be off to the vaults with you,' with which they all burst out laughing.

By this time Alistair was halfway down the stairs. He turned at the bottom and went down the last set onto the ground floor. He was lucky, Zeus was distracted and hadn't spotted him. He raced on and turned into the gallery where he had started his journey and saw that Nemean had found his way back. He raced through the seven-foot beings who were still walking around in discussion. He saw Jupiter and Heracles seated on the ground. They were eating grapes provided by Dionysus who gave one to Alistair as he raced past. Only Aphrodite, still headless, was standing up. She appeared to be barring his way to the exit with her good arm held out ready to embrace him. He slowed down in front of her but whichever way he turned she followed him. He heard her three companions counting him down, '1800, 1200, 500,' but it was impossible for him to get round her, and he froze as she placed her hand on his arm.

It was then that Alistair heard the voice of Mr Brown calling for him to get a move on. At the same time, Aphrodite and the scene behind her faded away from sight to be replaced by the figures in the gallery as we know them today. Alistair glanced at his watch: it read 6.01 pm.

In the years to come his abiding memory of the visit was of something mysterious having happened. However hard he tried he was never able to bring it fully to mind, nor could he explain how a green, grape-shaped, marble had found its way into his blazer pocket.

There are enough clues to enable you to follow Alistair's route through the Museum. However, from time to time exhibits are moved to different galleries. If you are unable to find any of the exhibits referred to in the story then please ask Museum staff to direct you to where they can be found.

More Letters from Beaumont Street

JACKIE VICKERS

16 Beaumont Street
Oxford
September 3rd 1915

Dear Edith

I was delighted to receive your letter announcing such good news. It arrived just as I was leaving for the station. Congratulations! To be a principal of a girls' school before the age of forty is quite an achievement and no doubt your insistence on studying at Somerville College was a bold step in that direction. I am sorry you have not had the occasion to revisit Oxford lately and I promise I shall ask Aunt Vera to take me to your alma mater (for, as you know, she has friends on the staff) so I can report back to you.

Do you remember my Aunt Vera? She married an Oxford don and it was both she and her husband who supported my wish to enter university, much to my mother's fury. The ensuing arguments caused a rift in the family, not yet healed. I never told you the whole story then, and cannot, even now, bear to revisit those dark days. Hubert has been strongly influenced by my parents and it has taken me twenty years to persuade him to allow me to visit Vera and revisit Oxford. Vera is only ten years older than I and in some ways has been like an elder sister.

From what I have seen so far, Oxford has changed a great deal in the twenty years since my first visit. In those days I wanted more than the life of a provincial wife and mother. You were very kind, offering me the encouragement I needed while showing you understood the mountain to be climbed! Well, I was not equal to the task. My mother was and still is a formidable opponent and she got what she wanted: a daughter who married well and two grandchildren.

But you ask for a full report on Oxford in wartime. My first impressions were of a veritable sea of khaki and black. There are soldiers everywhere and of those people not in uniform, many men wear black arm-bands and the women full mourning. On Wednesday Vera has invited me to spend the day with her. She regrets not to be able to offer me a room but the Belgian refugees they took in are still with her. Her daughter Lily's health gives her great cause for concern. However, her son William is flourishing and speaks of enlisting as soon as he is old enough, to Vera's great distress. I shall have more to tell you soon. Congratulations again on your new position.

Your loving friend, Maude

September 3rd 1915

Dear Mother

Hubert has told me of your kind offer to supervise

Frankie and Sybil in my absence. Sybil, as you know, is an enthusiastic and hard-working scholar; you need not be concerned on her account. Frankie, as you have already noticed thinks of nothing but the army and the war. I know you have his best interests at heart but this must not distract him from his studies.

Your loving daughter, Maude

September 3rd 1915

Dear Hubert

I should be very grateful if you could spend a few moments now and again to make sure Sybil is allowed the time she needs for her studies. Your daughter's interests do not always coincide with my mother's intentions.

I hope to spend time with Vera and her family soon. Her expectations are that we should meet as often as possible in the short time allowed me.

Your loving wife, Maude

September 4th 1915

Dear Edith

You can rest assured that your beloved Oxford has risen to the challenge; the men, young and old, have enlisted with enthusiasm. Of the three thousand undergraduates that filled the colleges, less than a quarter remain and those mostly underage, unfit or foreigners. Dons and professors are as eager to serve as the youngsters. Beaumont Street in particular throngs with men in uniform as Worcester College is one of the many that started officer training courses earlier this year. My landlady knows Balliol well and tells me it is more like a barracks now and their quad has become a drill square. She says her fellow lodging keepers are relieved to see, and house, so many volunteers, as they face difficulties, and in some cases ruin, with the dramatic fall in student numbers.

This morning I had something of a shock. Who should bring my breakfast but Tilly! Do you remember my mentioning her from my first visit? She is sadly changed and looks quite old and careworn though only a year or so older than me. Her husband was crippled in the Second Boer War and can only take on light work. One of her sons was killed at Loos, one is unfit for service and the other too young. I told her she must be very proud to have given such a fine boy to the cause, but she didn't reply and seems to be avoiding me.

I have spent all day revisiting old haunts, enjoying the luxury of having no-one else to consider. Trade here seems to flourish. Outfitters display uniforms, stationers sell black bordered cards and writing paper, small gifts and toy soldiers.

University buildings are everywhere converted to hospitals of various sorts. A tented hospital has sprung up in New College gardens and the Examination Schools has become the 3rd Southern General Hospital.

More later.

In haste, Maude

Tuesday September 4th 1915

Dear Frankie

I am sorry your grandmother has been raising your hopes of enlisting, for this war is not expected to last and as you are only fifteen you are certain to miss it. There is no harm in considering the different regiments and what would suit you best if you are still keen to have a career in the army. However, you may be interested that a school of aeronautics has been established in the University Museum here and the Royal Flying Corps is to be housed among eight of the colleges next year. There are plans afoot to build an aerodrome on Port Meadow on the outskirts of Oxford, next summer. So these are exciting times for those attracted to flying. Does it appeal to you?

Your loving mother

Wednesday September 5th 1915

Dear Edith

We visit Somerville in two days' time, so I expect to have much to report. I did not get the impression from your letter that you were aware of the latest developments in the College. Somerville has surpassed itself in its generosity; students and staff have moved to newly vacated buildings at Oriel College and Somerville buildings are now a hospital. They had less than three weeks for the move which was completed in May. They say Miss Penrose has been magnificent; the college is indeed fortunate in having such a remarkable woman at their head.

We hope to speak with some of our brave men, wounded in a fine cause. Hubert has kindly sanctioned the purchase of a few small comforts which I am to distribute, for Vera feels uncomfortable about it. I had hoped Tilly would advise, having been so near to such matters, but she only muttered that they were lucky to be alive. I tried to talk to her about the worthiness of sacrifice, the subject of a recent sermon at our church, but she said she had potatoes to peel.

Your loving friend, Maude

Wednesday September 5th 1915

Dear Hubert

Thank you for approving my suggestion of buying small gifts for the Somerville wounded. You may be sure I have taken note of your recommendation to be prudent in all expenditure.

Your loving wife, Maude

Thursday September 6th

Dear Mother

I am glad Frankie is such good company and that Sybil, even if you see little of her, is at least causing you no difficulties.

I saw Vera at last, yesterday. I wanted to treat her to lunch at the Randolph, for old times' sake, but she declined. Oxford may be full of officers in their smart uniforms, she said, but there is much want among families whose breadwinners have been killed or wounded. Consider how many warm socks can be bought for the price of one fillet steak. (Vera does much of her own marketing and cooking, so she is naturally more 'au fait' than I.) She and Thomas do much good and have taken in a Belgian refugee family. Oxford has been quite flooded with them. We lunched on cold cuts and salad together with the Belgian professor, his wife and four daughters. The parents speak tolerable, though heavily accented English and the girls only French, which Vera fortunately speaks so well. They are comparatively late arrivals, having travelled on a circuitous and frankly terrifying journey. The professor hopes to find employment soon, but Vera is not hopeful as his specialism is in Sanskrit and other ancient languages.

Lily is delightful, but so pale and wan that Vera fears consumption, though the doctors insist she has merely outgrown her strength. William is a splendid young man, full of patriotic fervour.

I wish you could accept that Vera truly had my best interests at heart all those years ago. It seems a pity to prolong your quarrel for surely Father would not have wanted this.

Your loving daughter, Maude

September 7th

Dear Edith

The Matron made an exception for Vera and showed us round the convalescent wards herself. All the nursing staff work long hours for as the fighting intensifies so the casualties increase.

Edith, this was the worst experience of my life. Not even the death of my father gave me such a shock, for these are all young men, some very young, barely eighteen. All the papers lead one to expect cheerful young heroes bearing their injuries with fortitude and even humour. But such injuries! There are men who have lost limbs, sometimes several – imagine! Others have lost their sight or have facial wounds too terrible to describe. Vera told me she saw William in every bed. We heard this morning that plans are being discussed to bring in conscription in the new year and then there will be nothing she can do to save him, for he will be eighteen at Christmas. Vera thinks of her professor and his family and is horrified at the human cost involved in supporting Belgium.

I find today's experience too distressing to describe in more detail.

Your friend, Maude

September 8th

Dear Hubert

I beg you not to encourage Frankie in his ambitions. Perhaps he could be made to see there is nothing honourable in taking another man's life. This slaughter will end, I hope, before he reaches eighteen and it would be a tragedy if he were to spend his life preparing and hoping for another conflict.

Your affectionate wife, Maude

September 9th

Dear Edith

You say you are too busy knitting socks and other comforts for the war-effort to spend time with any of the wounded. But I urge you to reconsider. These poor boys need visitors as they lie miles away from their families, many of whom lack the funds to travel here.

Yours in haste, Maude

September 9th

Dear Hubert

You tell me I know nothing of politics and nothing of business but I hope you will allow I know something about right and wrong. It cannot be right to send young boys in their thousands to be maimed and killed. Nor is it right for our family to profit from government contracts for khaki cloth for the army.

You have talked of having a billiard room and conservatory and car after the war and many more luxuries. But boys are paying with their lives and I want no part in it.

Maude

September 11th

Dear Edith

There is no more to be said, for we shall never agree. I am fully prepared to be a pariah in my community but perhaps my views will be understood and accepted long after you and I are gone.

It has been a long friendship – more than thirty years – but worse things can happen than suffering a difference of opinion.

Boys are dying, Edith, and mothers with sons are grieving.
Maude

September 11th

Dear Hubert

You say you donate liberally to 'good causes' but are too busy to be involved personally. You may know about profit and loss but what do you know about human suffering? Go to our nearest hospital and speak with an amputee or better still try to comfort some poor boy who has been disfigured and perhaps also blinded by flying shrapnel. Look into his eyes, if they still exist, see his pain and his fear of rejection. Tell me it never occurs to you that Frankie might one day share his fate.

Maude

September 13th

Dear Hubert

I'm sorry you find my letters 'eloquent but misguided' and my comments 'verging on the treasonable'. How can you possibly provide a convincing argument when your opinions are based entirely on hearsay and propaganda culled from the newspapers? Go to the station, if hospitals are not to your taste, and see the Red Cross trains discharging their tragic cargo.

You appear content to make excessive profits from this war and remain blind to the vast scale of death and destruction not experienced before in this part of the world. You ask when I mean to return home. Hubert, I am not coming home. I have my father's small legacy, I have modest but comfortable lodgings here and shall find work among like-minded people. There is a Quaker Meeting house in St Giles, not five minutes' walk from here; I intend to ask them for help.

Maude

Hubert – I am surprised that my 'pacifist tendencies' make you feel betrayed. I know what betrayal feels like more than most. I refer, of course, to the small matter of the trip to Paris in the company of your secretary some months before war was declared. Also the rather bigger matter of the closeness of your relationship with Mrs Ramsey.

It has just occurred to me that Mr Ramsey may not be aware of it. Isn't he responsible for arranging those lucrative government contracts?

Maude

Hubert – I am well aware of how the law stands regarding the custody of children. I am equally aware that public opinion carries a great deal of weight in our small town, particularly when it comes to the election of town dignitaries.

What would Sybil think of coming to live with me in Oxford? Do you know how she might feel about you and

Mrs Ramsey? Did you know Mrs Ramsey's daughter Evelyn is a good friend of Sybil's?

Maude

September 19th

Dearest Sybil

Your father does not wish me to communicate with you but I am anxious to put my side of things.

Quite simply your father supports the war and I do not. I have seen and spoken with many wounded soldiers and bereaved families in these last few weeks and now realise I was wrong to be convinced by patriotic rhetoric. Whatever happened to the commandment 'thou shalt not kill'?

I can no longer do what your father requires of me. The latest activity the ladies of our town were engaged in was the distribution of white feathers to all men of fighting age not in uniform. Any man who does not wish to kill is labelled a coward and I will have no part in this. Only devotion to the family has kept me in the North. Ideally I would have continued to suppress my personal feelings but this war has brought everything to a head. The rift between your father and myself widens by the day but I dearly hope to see Frank after the war. Boys tend towards fighting and guns, they do not see the consequences. I shall respect Frank's views and refrain from writing to him, painful though this might be.

Dearest child, I long to have you with me and though I can offer you only modest accommodation, rest assured there are good schools here and private tutors are easy to find now there are so few students left. Vera has been wonderful as ever and has told me she will happily correspond with you if you have concerns you wish to share.

I am anxious that your education be taken seriously. Your father and grandmother make no secret that they do not approve of your ambitions. In Oxford there is now an acceptance of women's right to an education; perhaps the tide has turned.

Sybil, I cannot forget the horrors I have seen and must follow my conscience. I hope and pray to have you with me soon.

I am sending this to your friend Evelyn in the hopes she will be discreet. Let me know your wishes soon.

Your loving mother

Sellotape and String

ANDREW BAX

A dishevelled old man struggles under the weight of a dusty packing case, dumps it on the reception desk, grunts and shuffles off. According to the block lettering on the outside of the case it once contained a vacuum cleaner, but it is now held together by sellotape, peeling and perished by age, and string. There is a little label on it: The Betty Becket Bequest.

The dishevelled old man is Betty Becket's son, Gilbert. It is unfortunate that Betty Becket had entrusted Gilbert with her bequest as he is unaccustomed to such responsibility; indeed, in a few days he recovers from a bout of heavy drinking with a suspicion that he should have delivered the packing case to the Bodleian but, by then, he is past caring.

The reception desk of the Ashmolean is staffed by part-time volunteers. Those on duty at the time are unprepared for dirty old packing cases and dishevelled old men so they just stare and say nothing. To their relief he leaves straight away, but the packing case is still on the desk and looks untidy. They put it out of sight on the floor, where it remains for another three weeks.

It is actually a cleaner who brings it to the attention of one of the museum's curators. The packing case is found to be full of spiral-bound notepads in which every page is covered in unfamiliar hieroglyphics. Initially, this causes a lot of excitement until one of the receptionists recognises them as shorthand. The packing case is closed up again, numbered, catalogued and put in a store-room, along with a large consignment of religious relics from Mongolia, boxed up in very similar containers.

It is discovered that Betty Becket had died the previous April at the age of 95. The only mourner for her at Oxford Crematorium was Gilbert, who arrived just as the curtain was being drawn across the coffin. She had lived in Rose Hill for some 20 years, and then in a care home in Littlemore. Gilbert is found to be a wholly dissolute character with multiple health and social problems. Neither he nor his mother appear in any academic records, so the Ashmolean's attention moves on to the Mongolian relics, whose provenance is now in considerable doubt.

At 10.45 pm on 21 September 1938 a future prime minister finally succeeds in enticing Betty Becket into his bedroom. She is just 17 and works in the kitchen of the country hotel where the future prime minister and other senior politicians have been having regular meetings away from the distractions of parliament. The arrangement with Betty becomes regular, and in a few months she is found to be pregnant.

The future prime minister fears the situation could wreck his career but he is a decent man. He has married well and is financially secure, so he rents a little house for Betty and arranges for her to be trained in secretarial skills so that she can have a career of her own.

Betty proves to be fast, accurate and discreet. The future prime minister recruits her to work in a secret government location where she advances rapidly through the clerical ranks and is soon taking dictation from some of the country's leading wartime strategists. With no particular object in mind, she numbers all her shorthand pads as they become full and keeps them, instead of throwing them away.

Some of the earliest pads provide clear evidence that Rudolf Hess, in his attempt to broker peace with Nazi Germany, was not acting alone. Contrary to official reports, the whole plan has been orchestrated by American intelligence who neglect to inform their British counterparts, resulting in considerable transatlantic tension. Memos in Pad No. 14 link this debacle to a controversial proposal from Washington that America, Britain and Germany should abandon the current conflict and form a new alliance to crush the Soviet Union. As a pre-condition, all German forces would be required to withdraw from Western Europe, a prospect which Hitler would not countenance.

In Pad No. 23, the name of the future prime minister appears for the first time, along with those of the highest officials in the secret location. Concern is expressed about Winston Churchill's taste for high living despite the straitened times. On 24 August 1944 (Pad No. 26) she is taking dictation from Churchill himself. There is a rambling memo, timed at 1.15 am, telling John Reith that, if he values his career, he should ensure that the BBC should NOT (in capitals) repeat rumours about contact with the Japanese. Two days later it seems the Germans have discovered the secret location, and bomb it, so the entire department, including Betty, are moved to some underground tunnels deep in the Chilterns.

Almost the whole of Pad No. 28 is taken up with the

minutes of a meeting on the professed neutrality of Ireland and how to deal with the problem 'once and for all'. In a conclusion likely to reignite the troubles so recently settled, it recommends that the Republic should be annexed. Overnight, known republicans in the North would be interned, while parachute troops would take over Dublin, Cork, Limerick and Galway, spear-headed by units of the Free French; it notes that the Americans could not be trusted in such a role. As the war draws to its end, a further meeting considers how to deal with the pressure for independence from India. The meeting covers several days and Pads 30 and 31 record a recommendation that Indian nationalism should be channelled towards its own imperialism with forces striking north through Afghanistan, Turkmenistan and Uzbekistan to take the oilfields of Kazakhstan. Such a move, the meeting notes, would have the additional benefit of destabilising a seriously weakened Soviet Union.

It can be deduced from the subject matter of correspondence beginning in February 1946 that Betty joined the staff of the Foreign Office. Whoever is dictating to her is intimately connected to the sale of jet engine technology to Russia. Later, there are memos headed Top Secret relating to the reliability of embassy staff around the world, culminating in a flurry of activity on the defection of Guy Burgess and Donald Maclean in 1951. Almost the whole of Pad 38 responds to allegations of incompetence in allowing these events to occur. And, despite protests, it seems that every member of the department, including Betty, becomes subject to MI5 surveillance.

However, Betty's reputation for absolute discretion must have persisted because she next appears in the Eden years. There are memos from Eden himself referring to a top-secret consignment of Russian bullion, sent to relieve the government's desperate financial plight, in exchange for certain positions being taken at the United Nations. The deal ends in fiasco when the consignment is intercepted by pirates off Sumatra, and strenuous efforts are made by the future prime minister to keep the story from the press. Later, there are details of a secret agreement for American funding of the joint British/French invasion of Suez on the understanding that, in public, the Americans would denounce it.

On 10 January 1957 the future prime minister achieves his ambition and becomes prime minister. One of his first acts must have been to bring Betty into No. 10 because there are letters confirming the appointment of his cabinet colleagues from the very day he took office. Their relationship was clearly private as well as professional because there are letters concerning his wife, Lady C, and her 30-year affair with Robert B. Intriguingly, it seems that Lady C comes to regard Betty as her private secretary as well. She makes persistent attempts to persuade Elvis Presley to appear at a charity ball to entertain her guests, but her main pre-occupation is to prevent the press from reporting on Robert B's bi-sexual behaviour. It can be gleaned from this correspondence that Robert B has fathered three children by different women while, at the same time, having a dalliance with a young cat burglar introduced to him by the gangster Ronald Kray.

Meanwhile the prime minister is deep in negotiations with the sub-Saharan colonies on their eventual independence, with crucial support from Canada. However, President Kennedy is set on building a ring of nuclear bases in

Canada's Arctic Archipelago enabling ballistic missiles to reach Moscow within 90 minutes. Notepads covering the early years of the prime minister's term of office show that he vehemently opposes this strategy; a deep and unreported rift between the two allies follows, resolved (Pad 43) only when he agrees to equip the Royal Navy with Polaris.

Pads 48 and 49 show that the murky world inhabited by Robert B is deeply involved in the blackmail of Vassall and the sale of naval secrets to Russia. Pad 52 contains a long memo from the prime minister on how the matter is to be presented to the press and his orders on how the truth is to be suppressed.

Although Pad 63 covers mundane matters, there is in it a letter from Lady C to the socialite Stephen Ward, thanking him for the wonderful party at Cliveden and saying what fun it was to meet the Keeler girl. She apologises for coming alone 'but my husband was too busy, as usual.' Within days the prime minister dictates a series of memos on the Profumo affair. Prophetically, Pads 66 and 67 contain hurried letters to friends and colleagues on his resignation. In them his anger at betrayal by his wife, the establishment and allies is evident. He promises to 'tell all' in his memoirs.

There is a gap of nearly a year before the notepads resume. The now former prime minister has taken the reins of the family firm, and Betty continues to be his trusted assistant. Much of her work concerns the humdrum world of commerce, but as the years pass she becomes increasingly involved in helping with the memoirs. There are letters to politicians, prime ministers and presidents around the world asking for clarification of certain facts and for their permission to mention matters which he knows to be true but which might cause some embarrassment. Of course, the notepads reveal only one side of the correspondence but much of it seems to attract a brisk and angry refusal. So, as the former prime minister is an honourable man, the eventual memoirs reveal nothing new. Only the notepads provide fresh insight into what really happened during those turbulent years.

It is December 1984 and Betty Becket, who lives alone, decides to cheer herself up by giving herself a Christmas present of a new vacuum cleaner, but waits for the January sales. She goes to the Comet Warehouse in Osney Mead and is amazed by the variety on offer. In the end, she chooses a red one and buys it for £11.99. She is delighted with everything about it, including the packing case which contained it. Just right, she decides, for all those notepads which she has been keeping for years but can't quite bring herself to throw away. By the time she has got them all in, the packing case is full; it could have been made for them. She seals it with sellotape, ties it up with string and, having a little joke with herself, she adds a little label: The Betty Becket Bequest. Then she finds room for it in the cupboard under the stairs.

Historians have often wondered about the work of the secretive Strategic Options Committee, tasked to think the unthinkable, for which there are no official records; indeed enquiries about the very existence of the committee are still met with a firm denial. But that is the organisation for which Betty worked for much of her career. Her notepads provide incontrovertible evidence of the range of actions considered in response to some of the major events of the time, actions that had a fundamental bearing on world events. They also confirm details of secret deals and conspiracies which have been long suspected, and discredit the existence of others. The scale of duplicity and brinkmanship which could have precipitated nuclear catastrophe is clearly documented. The Betty Becket Bequest is a primary source of even greater value than the official records.

Theresa May is the first prime minister to take office without the burden of responsibility for some unstable technology developed in the 1960s. Betty had been required to record the contingency arrangements for the rapid evacuation of everyone within a radius of 200 miles of the government research establishment at Porton Down. It was there that the prototype was dismantled with intricate and meticulous care over nearly five decades. The only person to discover its existence was an expert on biological warfare who died in mysterious circumstances near Longworth at the beginning of the Iraq War. On Betty's death, MI5 erased the matter from its files; but it didn't know about her notepads.

On less daunting matters, Lady C's contribution illuminates how the establishment saw itself and how it protected its own in difficult times. There is enough material in the notepads to keep social historians and investigative journalists in business for years. In the age of liberalism it was the rich who first turned to sex, drugs and rock 'n roll, and who were the first to be destroyed by them. Lady C has to deal with Robert B's nephew who, after squandering his own ample allowance, attempts to blackmail her by threatening to invite the Sunday newspapers to investigate the paternity of her eldest daughter. Even the social gossip in which Lady

C so freely indulged provides fascinating reading. Her spat with Madame de Gaulle would make tabloid headlines, even today.

These events took place half a century ago but they still have the potential to ruin reputations and attract lawsuits. The fact that they haven't is testimony to the power of a small group that had the capability to influence the courts and deflect police enquiries. And, of course, because no-one apart from Betty has read those spiral-bound notepads.

In September 2016, it is established beyond reasonable doubt that the Mongolian relics were actually crafted in the 1970s by a group of Kashmiri artisans. The donor's widow seems unsurprised by the news and has made it clear that she does not want them returned. Sturdy men in hard hats and reflective jackets are therefore summoned to clear the store-room and everything in it. They take the box of notepads too because no-one knows why the Ashmolean has been given it or by whom.

Some weeks later Gilbert is slumped in the waiting room of a clinic off Cowley Road, waiting for his Tuesday morning fix. Everything is being delayed because the hard-pressed staff are trying to calm a woman who is wailing in distress. It's as much as Gilbert can do to keep himself calm; he needs his fix badly. To distract himself he picks up an old magazine. Flicking through it, he notices an article headed *My Mum Sold PM's Secrets*. The 'secrets' seem to be about the domestic arrangements at Chequers, including what Harold Wilson had for breakfast. Even through his befuddled state it dawns on him: if that kind of stuff is sellable merchandise, what about all those notepads of his mother's?

The thought spurs him into action. Hauling himself out of the chair he stumbles towards Cowley Road. Just in time he catches a bus and dumps himself into a seat, almost on top of a little old lady who looks at him in alarm. He is starting to feel feverish and his heart is pounding. At the top of High Street he gets out and is nearly run down by another bus as he crosses Carfax into Cornmarket. Desperate now, he has to concentrate hard just to stagger along; he really should have stayed for his fix. It takes him ten minutes just to reach the Ashmolean. At the bottom of the steps he starts shaking but, with a huge effort, he climbs, falls and struggles on through the doors to the reception desk.

The sight of this bearded, bedraggled figure leaning over them stuns the two volunteers to silence. Gilbert mumbles incoherently about a box and someone presses a button discreetly located under the counter. Confusion follows. From the depths of his memory he manages to blurt out about The Betty Becket Bequest. Voices say they didn't know who he was or how to contact him ... only old shorthand pads ... cleared out weeks ago ... landfill. Muttering something about his fix, Gilbert sinks to the floor just as the police arrive to take him away.

Tour Diaries

ANNIE WINNER

Sarah   **October 3**   **London**

I got the part! My agent just rang to tell me. I can't believe
it. I've been to so many auditions in the last three months. I
was beginning to think I would never get work. It's a great
part – Isabel in *Long Nights, Happy Days.* Not the leading
lady, but I don't feel ready for that anyway. And it's a long
tour – six months – up and down the country. I wonder who
else is in it? The director is Aidan Jones.

Phoned Mum today to tell her the news. She's just back
from a week in Ibiza and was full of all the fun she'd had. She
seems to be having a second adolescence since she dumped
her last bloke and decided to concentrate on her female
friendships. Told Matt as well. I was a bit worried as he has
had hardly any auditions, let alone offers, and he's quite
competitive sometimes. He seemed OK about it though,
gave me a kiss and said he was pleased for me. I wonder if
he really is. I wish he'd stop lying around in our flat all day
and do something, get a job in a café or a bar, anything just
to keep his mind off things.

Frank   *October 6*   *London*
It's not a great part but thank God I got it. I can't say this to

anyone, even Jasmine, but I was beginning to think I would never work again. It's only in a touring production, but it's a six month tour. Sounds like the rest of the cast will be hot from drama school, all thrilled to bits with getting a part. It sickens me to see them thinking this will give them a future. It won't. It just leads to a lifetime of living hand to mouth. You watch your hair thinning and greying, your waistline expanding, your reviews seldom appearing in the best papers, and still you cling to the fantasy that this year you will make it; this year you WILL get that part in a West End musical, or East Enders, even CBeebies.

Not sure that I can tell Jasmine yet. I'll wait till after Christmas. I need to brace myself for her barely concealed scorn, although this time at least the job will be a long enough run to dent my overdraft.

Sarah   **January 2**   **London**

We started rehearsals today. Felt really nervous walking into that shabby little hall. Don't know why – it's not that long since I last did it. Clocked Celia Moss who I was at drama school with. She's playing Anna. But I didn't know anyone else. Some of them look a bit past it and I hadn't realised how ancient Aidan Jones is – he must be at least in his fifties.

Had a lovely Christmas with Mum and New Year with Matt's parents. I think they are really worried that he's still out of work.

Frank   *January 2*   *London*

Told Jasmine this morning. I had to really as I was up before she left for work. The first rehearsal starts at 10.30 today so she was surprised when I joined her for breakfast. She said – again

– that it was about time I made a contribution to our living expenses and that she's sick of being the only breadwinner round here. Told her it was a tour and I would be away most of the time, though sometimes near enough to London to be home occasionally. I could see she was welling up. I know why. She's been trying to get pregnant for months so we have to do it to order, at the right time of the month. Now I might not be here. There wasn't time to talk.

When I got to the rehearsal venue everyone else was already there – nine of us. Recognised Ida MacDonald, who plays the mother, although she's aged quite a bit. She gave me a big hug. But all the others looked like they were still in nappies, all eager and enthusiastic. Doesn't look like many of them have done much and several are fresh from drama school.

Sarah   **January 12**   **London**

Into the second week of rehearsals now and we open at the Marlowe Theatre in Canterbury early next month. It didn't go very well today. The guy who's playing Toby Mannering is weird. He's playing my sugar daddy but he reads the part like it's the football results. I get the feeling he really does fancy me which somehow makes it harder to act like it's mutual. No one's got their lines down yet, much to Aidan's annoyance. At this rate I can't imagine it will be ready by the end of next week.

It was fun in the lunchbreak though. Celia and two of the other girls are about my age, and we had a jokey time giving the blokes marks out of ten. The guy who's playing Toby Mannering came third, after Barnaby Gunne and Josh Richards. His name is Frank Darcy. He keeps himself to himself and has a superior air which we marked him down for. Apparently he was in Coronation Street for a year or two when he was young, but hasn't done much since. We shouldn't be so frivolous I know. Ida says he was quite something when she first knew him.

Frank   **January 26**   **London**

We are in the final week of rehearsals now. It's beginning to pick up a bit although the inexperience of most of the cast slows things down. One of the young ones, Sarah Fleming, is quite good and she's certainly got the looks. Lovely slim body with long legs, lots of curly, tawny hair. She's a bit full of herself though and giggles with the other youngsters in breaks, like adolescent schoolgirls.

Jasmine isn't speaking to me. Don't really know why. At least I'm home every night during rehearsals and you'd have thought she'd want to make the most of that given that I'm away on tour more or less all the time for the next six months. There are a few days between each stop and several week-long breaks when I could get home, but we're traipsing up and down the country on the usual illogical itinerary. The last one's Oxford, because Aidan keeps telling us that he'll take us all out to dinner at the Randolph after the final night of the tour. I remember it as a stuffy kind of place serving old-fashioned food. My parents took me there after my graduation. Somehow going to the Randolph helped them pretend I had been at the "proper" university rather than Oxford Brookes.

Sarah   **February 5**   **Canterbury**

Matt's got a job! Not acting, but he applied to be a teaching assistant post at the primary school round the corner and he got it. I know he's disappointed that he hasn't got an acting job, but at least this is regular money. Better than lying around all day not doing the washing up and playing endless games on his Xbox.

We're in Canterbury for a technical rehearsal tomorrow afternoon before the dress tomorrow night, with the preview the next day, then the first night. I'm terrified but so excited! Gina is doing really well in the leading lady role but Alan, her leading man, is still a bit wooden. Frank Darcy has warmed up a lot, and we've got quite friendly. Wish he wouldn't keep watching me though, it's a bit creepy.

Frank　　　　**February 8**　　　　*Canterbury*

The first night was a disaster. I lost concentration in the second scene, distracted by a glimpse of Sarah Fleming's breasts in her near transparent blouse, and fluffed my cue which rattled her and then Ida came in with the wrong line. Everyone wobbled then until we managed to get back on track. I don't think the audience noticed, although the applause was rather tepid. After the performance I found a Post-it stuck to my mirror from Aidan saying that he'd noticed the difficulty and was concerned about the pace, which made me feel more nervous than ever. But of course I can't tell him that – or anyone. I'm haunted by thoughts about Sarah – even dreaming about her, somehow chasing after me. Talk about wishful thinking. I even long to get back to Jasmine and safety. I'll be going home for the night to see her after the show on Saturday.

Sarah　　　　**February 12**　　　　**On the train to Liverpool**

Went home on Saturday night after the show. Frank Darcy was on the same train and came to sit opposite me which was annoying as I wanted to read my book. We chatted about the show and how it's going. He asked me what I thought about the mess up on the first night. I said I wasn't sure what happened but we seemed to rescue it fairly quickly. Then he said he'd fluffed his cue because he'd been distracted by me, which I thought was a bit much and not very professional. It's not my fault if he loses concentration. Then he went all pathetic on me and started telling me that his marriage was on the rocks and he wished he was free. Looking back I can't believe I even began to fall for that line, but at the time I ended up feeling quite sorry for him. He's not that bad looking for his age – Ida says he's the same age as her which I guess is late 30s. She won't say of course. At least he's still got hair and a waistline – just.

It was after midnight when we got into Victoria and as we both live in Finsbury Park we got on the tube together. I was going to text Matt to get him to come and meet me at the station, but Frank insisted that he'd walk me home. When we got to our block of flats he tried to kiss me – not just a luvvie peck on the cheek but a full smacker – and said he couldn't get me out of his head. I told him I was going home to my boyfriend. He looked shaken and said he didn't know I had one. It was well embarrassing.

Let myself into the flat half expecting Matt to be ready with a bottle of Prosecco, but he was in bed asleep so I crept in next to him and stroked him awake. After all, it was our last night together until the mid-tour break after Ipswich, although I'm trying to persuade him to come to Bristol for a couple of nights at the end of the run there.

Frank   *February 18*   *Liverpool*

Very different audiences in Liverpool. Or maybe I'm just feeling different after being slapped down by Sarah – well, not really, but she made it pretty clear she's not interested. It's quite hard being her lover in the play and trying to switch off from that for real life. I think she's been avoiding me, but the more I don't see her the harder it is to get her out of my head. She's there whenever I'm not thinking about something else. Her voice, especially her laugh, rings in my head; the way she tosses her hair over her shoulder, her habit of rubbing her eyebrow with her finger – all overrun my mind. It's getting worse all the time. I can't seem to get the situation in perspective. If only she was free, if only I was, I'd feel more confident to make a move, to make her want me. As it is I know I shouldn't be entertaining such thoughts, much less fantasising about what I'd have to do to get her.

Sarah   **March 10**   **Bristol**

Bristol is a great city. We (me and Celia) have been out walking round it, getting really fit as it's all up and down. Thank God we're in the same digs and Frank is in a different B & B. He keeps on gazing at me and it's really getting on my nerves. Told Celia about it. She thinks I should tell him to cool it but seeing as he's hardly actually said anything since that train journey I haven't got much to go on. I think Aidan's noticed something too – he was in the audience last night and asked me afterwards if everything was alright with me for no other good reason I could think of.

The tour is going well at last – we've had some good reviews and the show has often been sold out. It's Sheffield next, and then we've got a week off although my agent has fixed a couple of auditions. Can't wait to see Matt – he's coming on Saturday for the show. He's enjoying his new job. We Skype every afternoon and he's always got something interesting to tell me about work. He says he's really missing me. Same here.

Spoke to Mum today. She's got a new boyfriend. I don't know how she does it at her age – like I know she's well preserved, but she is 45. It must be exhausting having to get used to someone new yet again.

Frank   *March 17*   *Sheffield*

Tried to make sure I was on the same train as Sarah after the last night in Bristol. I'd arranged to go home for the Saturday and Sunday nights partly because I'd heard her telling her friend Celia that she was going to do the same. I prowled up and down the train but couldn't find her. Felt ridiculously disappointed. It was my only chance to get her alone – and I'd planned to make a real play for her. I can't stand it any longer – I've got to make a move, once and for all.

When I eventually got home I felt irritated with Jasmine who was all decked out in a sexy kimono affair which didn't turn me on at all. But she said she was ovulating so I had to perform. I should have been more honest and turned my back, but I got through it by shutting my eyes and pretending it was Sarah.

Jasmine kept asking what was wrong. How could I tell her? I just said I was tired and needed to sleep. She got more and more grumpy – can't say I blame her. What am I doing going along with this when I feel the way I do about Sarah?

Sarah   **March 18**   **Sheffield**

In Sheffield now. Managed to put weirdo Frank off the trail by letting him think I was going to London for the weekend after Bristol. What really happened is that Matt came down on Saturday for the last show in Bristol and we had a lovely night and day together before I got on the train with Celia to come up here on Sunday night. It was such a relief not to have Frank hanging around, always trying to be 'young' and gawping at me all the time. Matt said I was awesome in the play – it's the first time he's seen it. He is such a darling. I know he must feel envious of me doing well when he would really like to be doing what I'm doing, but he tries hard not to show it.

Frank   **April 4**   **London**

Jasmine thinks she's pregnant. I could tell something was up as soon as I got in – we've got a week's break from the tour. The train ride gave me a chance to think things through a bit. What is there left in my marriage? We've been together for 10 or more years and never had children – somehow the time has never been right. Either I've been out of work or Jasmine's next promotion or new job had been more important. Then when we were out for dinner on her 37th birthday she'd said she wanted a baby. I suppose I didn't mind and went along with it, but nothing happened. We settled back into me feeling I would give my acting one more chance – which never actually materialised anyway, at least until the current gig. Jasmine got more and more resentful at what she called my indolence, freeloading off her fat salary. Is there any coming back from where we are now? We can't even talk about it.

Should I tell her about Sarah? But what is there to tell?

Nothing has actually happened. I just can't stop fantasising about her. It's my default state of mind, imagining what we could enjoy together. Shouldn't really write my imaginings down in detail – they are pretty lurid. Could I live with myself if I abandoned the pregnant Jasmine to move in with lovely young Sarah? What would my parents think, our friends, my sister?

Sarah   April 7 London

Having a nice break at home with Matt, although it's odd him being out at work all day. We used to always be together during the day and I'm at a bit of a loss on my own. He seems to have lost interest in acting now and is talking of doing teacher training. We're planning to have a day out on Saturday - maybe a trip down the Thames to Greenwich.

Had two auditions this week. They didn't go very well, but we'll see. This tour lark is exhausting and I don't like being away so much. Matt doesn't seem so – well – ardent is the word.

Frank   April 26   Bradford

In Bradford this week, staying with an old-fashioned theatrical landlady called Sue, the sort who lets you have breakfast at 11 am, but expects conversation. I found myself telling her about Sarah and the situation with Jasmine. She said it sounded like I was terrified of the commitment a baby would mean and that my obsession with Sarah was an escape route. Just armchair psychology but I've found myself mulling that idea over.

Getting fed up with the others in the company. We're together too much and I don't have much in common with any of them. Even Ida and I have run out of old stories to share.

I've been speaking to Jasmine on the phone but we can't really talk – there's something getting in the way. Maybe that talk with Sue helped me to get things in perspective a bit. She might be right, that I'm just a commitment phobe looking for an exit route. It's strange how intimate and physically close I have to be with Sarah on stage, but in real life we hardly speak. I think she avoids me. Am I really too old for her? – not sure how old she is, but there can't be more than 15 years in it. I haven't really had a proper conversation with her since that time on the train all those months ago. I wonder about having one more attempt at telling her how I feel. I just don't know how to do it anymore, the declaration, the fear of what I'm pretty sure she'll say. I should probably message her on Facebook or something – I just feel completely out of my depth. Drowning.

Sarah   **5 May**   **Nottingham**

My agent called today. They want me for a second audition in a couple of weeks for a part in a six-part TV series! Awesome! Totally! In Nottingham this week but I've got to go to London and miss a performance, as we'll be in Exeter and it's too far to do there and back in a day. I called Aidan and he was very grumpy but agreed that my understudy can cover. I'll be able to see Matt which will be great as I haven't been able to get home for weeks, mostly because I can't afford the train fare.

All the others seem pleased for me, but there's always an undercurrent of envy. Well, I haven't got the part yet. This tour is going on too long; we're all fed up with each other. Called Mum to tell her the news but she doesn't seem that interested – just banged on about when am I going to come and meet her new man.

Frank is still stalking me. Whenever he walks in he looks around, looking for me, and then either turns away or looks miserable. It's horrible feeling watched all the time, but there's a bit of me that feels for him – he's quite sweet really and in a way I feel flattered. He looks so haunted and he's lost weight. Celia says she overhead him telling Ida that his wife is pregnant. You'd think he'd be pleased and want everyone to know, but he hasn't said anything to me.

Frank   *7 June*   **London**

Another week's break then thank God it's just Milton Keynes and Oxford and then this bloody tour will be over. Back at home with Jasmine who says she is ten weeks pregnant. I must say she is looking great and the ice she's doled out to me for the last few months seems to be melting a bit. We had quite a good talk about the baby and how things will have to change. She even suggested I stay at home with it when she goes back to work. Not sure that's for me but it's worth thinking about. Maybe there is something left to save. I seem to be assuming I'm staying.

Sarah has got a plum part in a six-part TV series – she's over the moon. Can't help adding a touch of jealousy to the fistful of feelings I have about her.

Sarah   **10 June** **Harlesden**

I haven't been able to write this for weeks. When I went down to London for my second audition I went back to the flat afterwards, thinking I would surprise Matt – he normally gets home from school about four. I let myself in and heard voices in the living room. I flung open the door and said 'Guess who!' to find Matt and this woman huddled together (too together) over the computer screen. He looked terrified when he saw me and the woman totally shocked.

Turns out she and Matt have been seeing each other for nearly two months – no wonder he seemed a bit cool when I was home in April. He claimed it was because I was never there and he was lonely.

I've been devastated ever since, totally, but couldn't tell anyone in the company, even Celia. I can't talk about it. I can't even write about it. Now we're on a week's break and I've had to stay with Mum and the ghastly Roger. He is decades older than her, fat, bald and drunk most of the time. What on earth have they got in common? She's probably lonely and he might be rich I guess.

Frank   *25 June   Oxford*

Thank God it's the last night tonight. I've had Toby Mannering, Long Nights, Happy Days, Sarah Fleming and all the rest of them up to the back teeth. I'm even looking forward to seeing Jasmine – I'm pretty fond of her really and I feel kind of protective about her. And having a baby will be fun; something new anyway.

The Playhouse has just had a refurb and the auditorium looks spectacular with its black and grey walls and velvet jewel-coloured seats – yellow, orange, dark blue, scarlet, burgundy. Hardly recognised it as the same seedy place I used to perform in when I was an undergraduate – don't think I've been back to Oxford since. Aidan said he was taking us all out to a meal after the show tomorrow instead of the usual end of tour party. Not to the Randolph as he'd promised but to some cheap place round the corner under Debenhams.

Sarah   25 June   Oxford

Found a lovely photo of me and Matt in the inside pocket of my overnight bag today. It was taken soon after we met. We were so in love. How can this have happened? Is the rest of my life going to be spent traipsing round the country, only seeing the people I work with and wishing I was at home with... whoever? Will I end up like Mum, living with some ancient has-been, a bottle ever open?

Frank   26 June Oxford

As we walked down Beaumont Street from the Playhouse to the restaurant last night after the final show of the tour, I was wishing I could be on my way home, but we'd probably be so late I'd miss the last train. It was a beautiful evening, a warm dusk had barely fallen. The elegant terraces of the street, trimmed with their intricate wrought-iron balconies, glowed in the twilight, and the grand columns of the Ashmolean still had the lovely radiance of Oxford stone. I fell behind the others, as usual having no particular friend to walk with. I felt a hand slip through my arm. It was Sarah's.

The Journal of Lady Claire de Boercy

JANET BOLAM

Set into a pillar on the north side of Beaumont Street at the Walton Street end, is a stone with the inscription: "Near to this site stood the King's Houses later known as Beaumont Palace. King Richard the Lionheart was born here in 1157 and his brother John in 1167".

This journal was discovered during excavations in the grounds of Worcester College, Oxford on the site of the now demolished Beaumont Palace.

It is a remarkably preserved record of events that took place in the year 1166. It appears to be written by a Lady Claire de Boercy (1123-1167), a close companion of Queen Eleanor of Aquitaine. Records first show that Lady Claire, daughter of Baron Guy de Boercy, was in attendance at the marriage of Eleanor to Louis, the second son of King Louis VI of France in 1137. She was mentioned in records of the Second Crusade, and was at Eleanor's side at her marriage to Henry, Duke of Normandy, soon to be King Henry II.

The journal was originally translated from the French and Latin by Professor Rodney Limpet, Professor of Medieval History at Fitzwilliam's College, Oxford, and adapted to Modern English by Susan Rose, playwright and dramatist.

***

Monday the 5th day of September, in the year of our Lord 1166
Poitiers

If one more member of the Court asks me 'Why must we go to Oxford?' I swear on God's Holy Bible, I will jump into the moat.

'The Queen has her reasons' I repeat and try to look knowing, although if truth be told, I don't know why either. Why, when she's with child – and no spring chicken – does she want to leave Poitiers where she is warm, safe and comfortable, to cross the dangerous Channel to cold, damp, miserable England? And why is she determined to spend her confinement at Beaumont Palace in Oxford? It's small and uncomfortable, and when she gave birth to Richard there not 9 years ago, she swore she would never return.

Mind you, she and the King have been arguing for weeks, ending with the most tempestuous row I have ever witnessed, and believe me, I have witnessed some battles in my time. I was with the Queen, deep in one of our late night discussions at the time and I can remember every word of it! The King was aflame, running up and down the hall screaming. At one point he actually grabbed his sword and began flailing it about. I was glad the rest of the court were not present to see this display, because frankly he was out of control, never a good thing for a King to be in my opinion. The Queen, to give her credit, sat calmly, her hands clasped on her lap. Only I knew it was to prevent them from shaking. Eventually, with a great roar, he threw the sword at the wall. I remember exactly what happened next.

'I repeat myself, Harry. Aquitaine should go to Richard.

Little Harry already has England, Anjou and Normandy. Our Empire ...'

'Our Empire is it?' he roared, 'never forget Eleanor, you may be my Queen, but you have nothing.' He put his face directly to hers, spittle, foul breath, sweat. But she waited until he moved away before she replied.

'You would have nothing if it weren't for me, and never forget it. Do you want our sons to war against one another because of unfair inheritance?'

'I'll say this one more time, Eleanor! I am the King, or do you need reminding of that? Harry, my eldest son needs land and wealth behind him if he's to carry on my legacy...'

'...our legacy.'

'MADAM YOU OVERREACH YOURSELF'

Or words to that effect.

Tuesday the 6th day of September, in the year of our Lord 1166
Poitiers

Last night was like the old days between Eleanor and I. We are, after all, sisters in all but blood. I was by her side when her dear father died and King Louis VI of France, who was supposed to be her guardian, immediately married her off to his son, who soon became king himself. We both hated the French court – too serious by far, but not nearly as bad as the Crusade. Eleanor was forced to follow her husband the King, and I will never forget the heat and the flies and the blood as we rode for Jerusalem. It was she and I, together, who planned the annulment of her marriage to Louis and her swift marriage to the young Henry. It is this long strong history together that ties us so close. She knows I would give my life for her, not just because she is my Queen, but because she is my friend.

Late last night, close in her chamber, when the Palace was silent, when we felt safe from Henry's spies, we took stock of the situation and planned her next steps.

The next section of this journal is missing. History tells us Eleanor went to Rouen to see her mother-in-law, Queen Mathilde. To make peace or declare war, we know not.

Tuesday the 1st day of November, in the year of our Lord 1166
Barfleur, Normandy

I am exhausted. It is chaos here. You can hardly see the dock for the crates, boxes and pallets, but finally the boats are loaded and the Queen is installed. The number of people we must take with us is necessary, but it all adds up. We have all the royal children and their retinue with us (bar Prince Harry, for the King insisted he stayed with him in Aquitaine), a whole school of advisors, guards, standard bearers, and the Queen's personal courtiers, including every troubadour and entertainer we could summon at such short notice. Then we have the necessary provisions. I for one could not face a cold English winter without some figs, dates, and oranges, some wine from Anjou – I cannot abide mead – and almonds, plenty of almonds. We are like a small army. Surveying the frantic activity at the dockside, it occurred to me that this is the court of a Queen preparing for exile in all but name. It makes me shudder, but I remind myself, as I reminded Eleanor last night, that there has been bitter argument before and there has always been a way back from the brink. Why should this be any different?

The sea is quite calm and I thank the Lord for that, but the priest can't say enough prayers for us as far as I'm concerned.

***

The only time I will ever sail across that sea again is when I return home. On that subject, I will say no more.

Saturday the 12th day of November, in the year of our Lord 1166
Woodstock, Oxfordshire

I haven't had a chance to record my thoughts for weeks because we've been traipsing around from castle to castle, travelling north, south, east and west, meeting the English nobles, and parading through one dreary English town after another, and I haven't had a moment to myself. The Queen, always mindful of her duty, wanted to visit as many nobles as possible and to be seen by as many common people as she could. So, despite the weather, which is always cold and damp, we rigged ourselves up in our finery and had the horses groomed to within an inch of their lives. We certainly made a spectacle as we rode through towns and villages, scattering the bales and bales of lavender and dried herbs brought from Provence as we passed by. In Banbury, the troubadours played in the marketplace. I swear every woman and girl swooned when Maxim sang his version of **Douce Dame Jolie**. Maxim is blessed with the most handsome face and a singing voice that melts the hardest of hearts.

Why do we do this? I ask myself this question every morning without fail. My limbs are stiff and my skin is red and sore from the bitter winds I must endure. I'm certainly not as young as I was. I have to remind myself at regular intervals that the Queen is managing all of this with vivacity and charm. At the end of the day, when I am sitting with my feet in a pail of water, the Queen is still at work with the protracted business of government, resolving disputes between nobles, ensuring Henry's interests are served. Her style is to use her beauty and charm and the comforts of her court to seduce the wary Lords and Ladies of England who had so recently suffered dark days of revolution and misrule. She is most certainly a master in the art of diplomacy and the King should never forget it, in my opinion.

I often ask myself, why does she do this when she and Henry are secretly at war with one another? The answer, of course, is she does it to secure the future for her children and through her children, she secures her own future. Also, the King holds Prince Harry as an unsuspecting and innocent hostage. King Henry knows that Eleanor will remain loyal to him as long as he has their eldest son by his side, or as good as, since he is now with his Grandmother in Rouen. Few people – and I count myself as one – can understand the true delicacy of the balances at play.

***

Disaster struck on our way to Sudeley Castle when the Queen was thrown from her horse. She shouldn't have been riding her own horse in the first place in her state – she is huge with child – I mean huge – and you can never be too careful, but try telling Eleanor that. Fortunately, the court physician would brook no argument, and insisted she took some rest. Woodstock Palace was a short ride away so we made our way there without delay. The physician was worse than useless, so with the help of my maid, Marie Anne, I brewed a potion from some of the dried herbs we'd brought from France. They did their work well and the Queen regained her health quickly.

What a relief it is to settle into such luxury! You can barely believe it was once a hunting lodge. Tapestries worthy of Anjou, comfortable places to sit, warm fires, bedchambers aplenty, and I believe there are the most exotic gardens hiding under the blanket of snow. I begin to hope the Queen will choose to stay here for her confinement after all.

Monday the 14th day of November, in the year of our Lord 1166
Woodstock, Oxfordshire

We learned today why this palace is so grand. It is in honour of one of Henry's mistresses, a girl, a nobody, named Rosamund Clifford, who is living here at the King's behest! We discovered this quite by chance. Maxim, an old hand in the realm of love, was romancing Lady Violet, the daughter of Sir Thomas, the squire who is responsible for the upkeep of the palace. She told him how they smuggled Rosamund – who, by the way, Lady Violet suspects is also with Henry's child – away to Godstow Priory as soon as they heard the Queen was coming. By my reckoning, they must have packed her up and shipped her off within an hour – quite a feat.

Now, this is not the first time the King has taken up with some young, ambitious girl and it won't be the first of his bastards, but just look at this finery and elegance! Just think how much this will have cost the King, and all behind Eleanor's back! Rosamund must mean much more to him than the average mistress. The thought turns sour like wine turns to vinegar. The Queen kept her own council, but last night she gathered her children around her and held them close. We leave for Oxford at first light.

Saturday the 19th day of November, in the year of our Lord 1166
Beaumont Palace, Oxford

Good news. Prince Harry is on his way to England. When we left Poitiers, Henry was adamant that their eldest son should stay with him to 'learn the art of hunting'. A shallow code. By keeping him in France, Henry secures Eleanor's loyalty despite their disagreements, so allowing little Harry to come here must be a sign that the ice is thawing. Maybe there will be peace between them before long? I cautiously thank the Lord. The Queen announced a banquet in honour of her son's arrival, despite the fact that we are being abstemious for Advent. It's just as well because the court becomes jittery and bored when we are hungry, and then all manner of mischiefs stir.

Walking from the Chapel after Morning Prayers the Queen told me she intended to invite Rosamund to the Palace. I said thought it a bad idea and that I doubted she would come, whereupon Eleanor drew herself to her full height and declared that she would obey if her Queen summoned her. Furthermore, just to make sure there is no misunderstanding, she ordered me to issue the invitation myself and to return with her the same day. I don't take kindly to being treated like a servant, but I am curious. It's a good job Godstow Priory is a short boat-ride from here because it has started to snow quite heavily and I am a creature of the sun. How I miss fertile, green Poitiers.

Saturday the 26th day of November, in the year of our Lord 1166
Beaumont Palace, Oxford

To describe Lady Rosamund Clifford as a beauty does her an injustice. She has a translucence and vulnerability about her that draws people in like moths to a flame. But I am not fooled. I can see what a manipulative little madam she is. She gives herself away by the look in her eye when she thinks no one is watching. I saw that look last night at dinner. One of haughty triumph as I was obliged to give up my customary seat within the royal party to allow Rosamund to sit next to the Queen. They spent the whole evening deep in conversation – they even shared oranges. Rosamund turned her head, and our gazes locked. It was she who broke away first, but it was too late for her to hide. I could see the flinty calculation in those dazzling blue eyes. I have your measure Rosamund Clifford; never believe you can outwit Eleanor, the Duchess of Aquitaine and Queen of England. Not with me by her side to defend her.

The bevy of accompanying nuns, who are, after all, just homeless girls who have been thrown out by their own families, are ecstatic to have a brief time free of that claustrophobic Priory and they are discovering the joys of mead. Hardly the reliable guards the Abbess intended. To add to the merriment, the Queen has called upon the troubadours to perform at supper, and I can't help noticing that Maxim is being particularly bold. For example, he sang a song of love to the Queen, but according to those seated nearby, he allowed his eyes to turn to Rosamund, who blushed deeply. Eleanor appeared not to notice. It was then I knew it was a plot, but really so obvious and so unworthy of the Queen. I am fully aware of Maxim's charms, they have seduced many a lady, but this clumsy attempt to undermine Rosamund's reputation is risable, and I wonder who advised such a course? Mind you, Maxim has never failed to seduce a woman if he sets his mind to it. Take it from one who knows.

***

Over the past weeks, the Queen has favoured me less and less. Just a month ago, I would have been party to her thoughts, but now I am left to speculate like a gossipy lady of the Court. All in all, I am very worried about her and wonder if being with child is taking its toll. She has huge rings under her eyes and her temper is very short. This morning I went with some dried figs to see if their sweetness would help, but all I got was a mouthful of venom. She's never spoken to me like that before. Her maid told me she isn't sleeping well, but still! I think Eleanor is more unnerved by the presence of that little trollop than she lets us know.

Sunday the 27th day of November, in the year of our Lord 1166
Beaumont Palace, Oxford

The big excitement of the day is the arrival of Prince Harry. He has brought all manner of goods with him including huge crates of oranges, almonds and raisins thoughtfully sent by Queen Mathilde. We're so excited to bring some French sunshine into this grey English winter.

Late last night, I tried to see the Queen in her bedchamber. In the past this has been the time and place where we talk to each other as equals, but my way was barred and I was told she was too tired to see anyone. I can't think how I may have offended her and I wonder what I must do to restore normality. I find this very distressing indeed.

As I prepared for bed, my maid Marie Anne distracted me with some interesting gossip. Apparently Maxim is in real turmoil. For the first time in living memory, a lady he has decided to court has rejected him. And who is the lady in question? Rosamund, of course. At least she has the sense to spurn him, but the Queen's plan, if it was a plan, has failed just as I expected. I slept very badly again.

Thursday the 1st day of December, in the year of our Lord 1166
Beaumont Palace, Oxford

The Queen continues to exclude me and I am at the point of despair. She looks pale and strained and is clearly struggling with this child she carries. She has refused my help more than once in the past few days. I spent a good hour in prayer, trying to fathom out what I may have done to offend her.

Only small fragments of the next few entries exist but it can be seen that Lady Claire visited Oxford Castle and then a Priest who lived near St Giles. The Priest was well known for his herbal remedies.

Sunday the 4th day of December, in the year of our Lord 1166
Beaumont Palace, Oxford

Finally, it's the day of the Banquet. We are doing it in the French style, of course, which confuses the English. In the Great Hall the trestles are covered with white cloths, ready and waiting for the platters of oranges and almonds, and the hogs and swan and peacock that are roasting as I write. The smells from the kitchen of the meat and spices catch the air. Cardamom, ginger, cumin. Ah! How they remind me of home. How I ache for a sunny afternoon beside the river Loire.

The guests include some surprises. Thomas Beckett comes uninvited, he who has been riding at the King's side as his close

*advisor for some time now. I wonder why he's here if not to spy
for the King.*

There follows pages that are illegible. Fragments show that
she describes the banquet in detail, what was consumed, the
songs and the dancing.

Monday the 5th day of December, in the year of our Lord 1166
Beaumont Palace, Oxford

*I was woken by my maid at first light. Rosamund was very ill,
so naturally I hurried to her side. She was green and weak from
retching and was far more affected than I had anticipated, but
even so, she still carries her baby. The nuns were up in arms
declaring foul play, of course. On my way back to my rooms,
I was intercepted by Thomas Beckett who demanded to know
what was happening. Now, this Beckett is dangerous. He has
more intelligence than many men, and he has the ear of the
King, so if he suspected Rosamund had been poisoned, the
news would reach the King by the speed of a raven, and the
consequences for Eleanor would be unthinkable. I managed a
sweet smile, 'I can only assume she was a silly girl and drank
too much wine.'*

   *'Not a drop passed her lips. She only drank the juice of
oranges,' he returned gravely.*

   'How can you be sure of that?'

*Beckett didn't answer and I was left to my own conclusions.
Worrying.*

   *'She'll be as right as rain by sundown, you wait and see.' I
tried to sound bright and confident, far from how I was really
feeling. 'To change the subject for just one moment,' I continued,*

'are you aware that the Queen is with the Earls Leicester and Gloucester and they seem to be in deep conversation?'

'Is she? Are they?' Beckett was immediately alarmed. This was something he needed to be a party to. 'Perhaps I'll go to join them.' And off he trotted like an obedient hound. Men. So predictable. I only hope it has distracted him for a few hours and I pray that Rosamund survives for all our sakes.

Tuesday the 6th day of December, in the year of our Lord 1166
Beaumont Palace, Oxford

Rosamund finally lost her little bastard in the early hours of the morning. I have dispatched Marie Anne to give her anything she needs to aid her recovery. I can't wait for her to go back to Godstow, Woodstock, or wherever, and for her to take her pack of wailing, drunken nuns with her. At least she no longer carries the King's child.

I gave Marie Anne seven silver coins in thanks for her discreet service.

Thursday the 22nd day of December in the year of our Lord 1166
Beaumont Palace, Oxford

The Queen summoned me in the dark hours of the night.

'If I had wanted Rosamund poisoned, I would have done it myself,' she whispered close to my ear, 'but I am not a fool. I did not ask for it, nor did I wish for it. You don't understand as much as you think you do.' She paused for a moment, then suddenly she kissed my cheek.

'You are a loyal friend, and for that I thank you, but I must know the truth, Claire, and from your own lips.' She looked at me with her pale puffed up face lit by a single candle. I knew *then she was in possession of enough evidence to know the truth.*

'I did it for you,' I whispered. 'The child she bore would always be Henry's love child and I feared for your own children. But you must believe me, I would never have let her die. I would never have done anything that could cause you harm. I swear by all that is good and true, I would never do anything to harm you.' She nodded slowly. Tears ran down her face. Then we knelt in prayer together, side by side, just as we were on the day we fled Poitiers, just as we have been all our lives, and my love for her swelled to fill my whole being.

Upon my right side I me lay;
Blessed lady, to thee I pray:
For the tears that ye lete
Upon your sweet son's feet,
Send me grace for to sleep,
And good dreams for to meet,
Sleeping, waking, till morrow day be.
Our Lord is the fruit, Our Lady is the tree,
Blessed be the blossom that sprang, Lady, of thee.
In nomine Patris et Filii et Spiritus sancti.
AMEN

The journal of Lady Claire de Boercy ends here. Records show she died of a fever on the Twelfth Night. Prince John was born on December 24th 1166 (not, as previously supposed, 1167).

Let No Man Put Asunder

GEOFF BREMBLE

Her side of the church had been starkly empty of people except for the few new friends she had made since moving here. The best man's speech had been a brilliant combination of humour and acceptable smut, but marred by a crass remark about the bridegroom not having to worry about keeping the peace with the in-laws. It was only his Gran who had observed the look on his bride's face, not one of offended sorrow but of deep, dark thunder, no sooner there before it had gone.

'There's something not quite right about her,' muttered Gran to no-one in particular.

For him though, the day had been all that he could have wished for: the church looking perfect under a light dusting of snow, a clear blue sky and all his friends and family there.

They had met six months previously through an online dating agency. He had been attracted by her ghostly elf-like features and piercing green eyes set in a face framed by flowing locks of jet-black hair. When they subsequently met, he was intrigued by her quiet demeanour but he had also detected an underlying sadness which made him feel deeply protective towards her.

It was early evening two months after they had met when, walking down Beaumont Street on the way to her place, it had started to rain. As fortune would have it they found themselves passing the Randolph Hotel, which neither of them had ever been into and which they knew only by reputation.

'Come on, let's go in here out of the rain. I've always wanted to try it.'

'Do we have to?' she had remonstrated.

'We'll be alright. Just the one drink while it stops raining.'

'But isn't it very expensive?'

'Yes, but don't worry I can afford it.'

They then mounted the steps and stood hesitantly in the foyer, wondering what to do next. To their surprise they were rescued by a smartly attired member of staff wearing a black knee-length coat, black trousers and a black tie set against a crystal white shirt, all finished off by a black top hat.

'Can I help you?' the concierge asked politely.

'Yes pal. Where's the bar?' was his response.

The concierge, although surprised by the abruptness of the reply, retained his professional composure.

'Certainly sir, come this way and I'll find you a table.'

They followed him into the lobby before turning left where they were greeted by a sea of chattering people – early evening drinkers en-route home, elderly theatre goers having a pre-theatre snifter before moving next door to the Playhouse – and all amidst a scattering of hotel guests, many of them clearly from foreign lands. But what struck them most was that with all these people in the bar the noise was nothing like they had experienced before. It was not the raucous sounds that they were used to; it was a more restrained atmosphere against a backing of light orchestral music. They were taken to a table in the farthest corner of the room closest to the bar, all the while conscious of being the centre of attention of the assembled drinkers. The concierge gestured to them to sit down, first pulling out her chair and once she was seated providing the same service for him.

'The barman will be over to take your order,' he advised them.

'It's alright mate, I'll go to the bar.'

'I'm sorry sir, you have to wait to be served,' was the concierge's somewhat sharp response, after which he went back to his allotted place in the foyer.

'Well that put you in your place,' she said with a laugh as they settled in.

'Bloody stupid system,' he grumbled.

It was then that a second barman, whom they hadn't spotted, came over and handed them the wine list while greeting them with,

'Good evening sir, madam, welcome to the Randolph. I'll give you a couple of moments for you to decide what you would like to order.'

Taking charge of the wine list, he leafed through the pages and then put it down on the table and turned to her.

'I'm going to have my usual pint of Guinness, what would you like?' he questioned.

'A large glass of house white,' she responded with a somewhat reluctant sigh, 'as usual.'

He then called the barman over and, holding his gaze, gave him their order. They lapsed into silence for a minute or two while taking in their surroundings. It wasn't long before he got tired of waiting.

'Where's the bloody drinks?' he said belligerently, 'I told you so – I'd be on me third pint if they'd served me at the bar.'

It was then that he sensed the returning barman behind him.

'I'm sorry if the speed of our service is not to your liking sir, I'll be sure to mention it to the manager,' was his response as he placed the drinks on their table before moving back behind the bar.

'Oops, I don't think he likes you and if you go on like this we're going to get thrown out,' she commented with a grin.

It was then that he spotted two photographs on the wall behind her.

'Hey look,' he exclaimed, 'isn't that the Morse bloke from the telly?'

'Where?' she said looking round the room expectantly.

'Not there, behind you, the photo,' was the response, 'but I don't know who the bloke above him is.'

She twisted around.

'Oh yes, I like him,' she said, 'and the man above, he's Colin Dexter. He wrote the stories and he's always in at least one of the scenes on the telly.'

'Oh yes, you're right.'

'I know I'm right,' she responded facetiously, 'and cheer up, I'm beginning to like it in here, it's warm and cosy.'

The tension of coming into this place was broken and they burst out laughing before picking up and clinking their glasses.

'Cheers!' they said in unison before he carried on, 'you're right and, as we've managed to get in here and it's pissing down outside, we might as well make a night of it.'

As the evening went on and the wine and Guinness took hold he opened his heart about his feelings for her and about them living together. At this suggestion she at first went quiet, then she gripped his hand tightly and started to talk in a low whisper.

'Please stop, I think there's things you ought to know before we agree to live together. I'm an only child and my parents, my grandparents, they've all passed on. I was orphaned on the eve of my twelfth birthday when the cottage we lived in was struck by lightning. The thatch caught fire – my father got me out and went back to rescue my mother but…'

She couldn't go on and clung to him sobbing into his shoulder as he held her in a tight embrace.

'You poor thing, and your grandparents; where were they, were they there as well?'

'No, thank God and they took me in. They were well into their seventies and didn't really know what to do with me, I made their life hell.'

She paused, then pulled away from him in an attempt to compose herself.

'I don't know how to tell you,' she managed to choke out.

'Tell me, tell me what?' he questioned in alarm.

'I was all mixed up, went with the wrong crowd – expelled from school and escaped to London. I moved into a squat – drugs and thieving were all we did but I was lucky, didn't get caught.'

Shocked by this revelation he felt a churning in the pit of his stomach and, looking into her eyes, he could sense her fear of rejection.

'But you couldn't go on like that. Why didn't you get a job?'

'I couldn't, I was in too much of a mess. But then my grandparents, they passed away, left me all they owned, money, the house, the lot,' she responded, her whole body convulsed with emotion.

'How did anyone find you to let you know?'

'My mobile, I rang my Gran occasionally. So I returned home, pulled myself together, got a job and then fell in love with a wonderful man.'

'What was he, what did he do?' he asked anxiously.

'He was a lorry driver, worked all over Europe. He moved in with me and soon after that I became pregnant,' she said, her voice so choked with pain that he could hardly make out what she was saying. He took her hand.

'Where is he now? Why aren't you with him? And the baby?'

'He's dead, killed in a pile up in France. I couldn't handle it – started drinking again and then, I lost the baby.'

She couldn't go on until, with great tenderness, he was able to give her the courage to continue.

'I fell apart, drink and drugs, sold the house, spent all the money, moved back to London, took up with the old crowd – drink, drugs, prostitution, you name it I did it again.'

'But how could you, not after what happened last time?' he remonstrated.

She looked up at him, her eyes pleading for understanding.

'Believe me it wasn't easy. I had lost all hope that I could ever be happy again, but then I lost my only real friend to heroin; it brought me to my senses. I moved here, dried out, got a job, met you, and now I have you. I do have you, don't I?' she pleaded as she wiped away a tear.

'Of course you do, and forever.'

They clung on to each other, her confession serving to cement their love, and he made the decision that whatever lay ahead he would protect this beautiful, delicate woman.

It was then that he proposed marriage, her response being a tearful, 'Yes, oh yes,' as she dug her nails hard into his hand.

By now his eyes were red with tears, her face streaked with mascara; he reached for his handkerchief and wiped her face gently.

'I think we need another drink,' he said looking at their empty glasses, 'how about a bottle of Champagne to celebrate?'

And so, only four months after they had pledged their lives to each other they had knelt before God and he had heard those words that would never leave him:

Those whom God has joined together let no man put asunder.

But now, only a month after that perfect day, the tragedy of her life had been revealed as a sham. However hard he tried, he couldn't get this mocking phrase out of his head. He found himself back, seated in the same pew in the church where the ceremony had taken place, asking himself the question he couldn't answer.

'How has it come to this?'

Apart from needing an answer to this question, he wasn't sure why else he was there and so, after a few minutes, and not having found any other comfort in the all-enveloping silence, he left. He then took himself even further back in time to the place where she had so ruthlessly drawn him into marriage. And so for the second time he was seated in the Randolph, this time drinking whiskey ice and not the fabled Black.

He asked himself again, 'How has it come to this?'

But again he got no answer, and so after a few whiskeys he moved round the corner to the Gloucester Arms, his regular drinking hole.

It was around five thirty; there were just three other drinkers in the bar and Queenie, the landlady, was sat on a stool at the far end, idly flicking through the evening edition of the *Oxford Mail*. She paused, seeming to be about to engage him in conversation as she usually did, but then appearing to think better of it she folded the paper and moved it out of sight on the ledge beneath the bar. He too had the newspaper in front of him, on which he had placed a sealed envelope addressed to him, together with a copy of the *Daily Mirror*. In his right hand he was firmly holding a whiskey glass, the ice that had clunked so confidently into it ten minutes previously now melted. He would have liked a cigarette but he would have had to go outside for that and he still had a decision to make.

He finished his drink and tried unsuccessfully to get Queenie's attention; it seemed clear that she wanted nothing to do with him. It had now gone six and behind him the pub had been slowly filling up with workers, and all the stools except the one next to him had been filled. Suddenly an arm and a body pushed past his shoulder and sat down. He was a big man, unshaven and with a mane of untidy greying hair, well over six foot and clearly able to handle himself. But not threatening, except maybe when crossed and with a few beers inside him late at night.

'Alright if I sit here?' he asked, in a distinctively northern accent.

'Yes, sure,' was the response.

The newcomer called over to Queenie. 'Hey girl there's a bloke here trying to get another whiskey, looks as if he really needs one, and I'll have a pint of Guinness.'

He turned back to continue the conversation he had started.

'You a local?'

'Yes.'

'That's good. I'm meeting some mates here; they're coming off the bus from Liverpool for the match tonight and we need to know how to get to the Kassam Stadium, any ideas?'

It was then that the newcomer spotted the *Mirror* lying on the bar.

'Hey pal, g'is a borrow. See if me gee-gees have come in,' he said leaning over.

'Help yourself,' was the unnecessary reply. Then, as the newcomer grabbed the paper, he saw the news item that dominated the open page, comprising a headline that read 'The Lottery winner and the Bride from Hell' with, underneath it, a photograph of two people on their wedding day.

'Wharr about that then, the poor bastard. Mind you, I wouldn't kick her out of bed – she looks a bit of a goer.'

He paused, staring at the faces on the page, then leaned forward and turned in order to get a good look at him.

'That's you, innit? It's you!' he uttered in total disbelief.

'Yeah, it's me,' came the confession.

'Bugger me. Hey, sorry about what I said about her before, it just slipped out. Even so you must be a bit of a dickhead gettin' caught up with the likes of that, tasty or not.'

'Yeah, you might say so.'

'But why did she finger you, you got loads of money or something?'

'Yeah, won the lottery.'

'With money like that it seems to me like you could have taken your pick, I mean she's been around the block a few times hasn't she?'

'I didn't think so at the time and when she's painted up she's a real looker, couldn't take me eyes of her.'

'But how'd you get caught?'

'Never saw it coming, gave me a load of crap about being an only child.'

'And she wasn't?'

'No, the youngest of six. Then told me her parents were dead, killed in a fire.'

'And they weren't?'

'No, both still alive, no blazing inferno, and even her bloody grandmother is still alive and kicking. She'd told me she was dead as well.'

'You want to be careful, she might want to kill you off.'

'Not funny. Then she told me her husband had been killed in a crash and she'd lost a baby.'

'Not true, I guess.'

'No it's bloody not. Kids, she's got three of the little buggers and no dead husband, just one divorced and then all the others.'

'Bloody hell, anything else?'

'Yeah, claimed she was an alchy, got into drugs, went on the game.'

'Well I'd have run a bloody mile after all that. What made you marry her?'

'She said that my love for her had saved her from her wicked ways.'

'Christ, and you swallowed all that. You're a bloody idiot. Did she manage to get her hands on your lottery money?'

'No, thank God. She wanted us to have joint accounts but I said no then bang she's gone, no note, no nothing, like she disappeared off the face of the earth. Now here she is, large as life, a full-page spread in the *Daily Mirror* and another one in the *Oxford Mail* – the two of us side by side outside the church, her all dressed in bloody white.'

'You poor bastard! Anyway, look on the bright side, the *Mirror*'ll pay good money for your story. You ought to get in there before she does.'

'They've already got her story. They phoned me for mine and I reckon that envelope contains an offer for it.'

'Well, what you waiting for, go ahead – open it.'

'It doesn't matter what's in there, I'm not going to give them my side of the story.'

'Does that mean you still fancy her? Get real pal, she's a waste of space, cash in while you can. After all Lottery or no Lottery you can never have enough money.'

As the newcomer was saying this he picked up the envelope and quickly opened it.

'Christ, that'll buy a few bevies but you want to bargain for more; after all it's not every day you get a story about a serial... eh, what's the word?'

'Bigamist.'

'Yeah, a bigamist, and says here she'd been married seven times before she married you.'

'Yeah.'

'And they were all named Henry.'

'Yeah.'

'And, let me guess, your name's Henry. So that makes you...'

'Henry the eighth,' they said in unison.

Then a roar across the bar, his mates had arrived.

'Hey fellers, come over here, meet Henry, Henry the eighth! He's got a bit of a story to tell, he's loaded and he's buying.'

'Bastard,' was all Henry could mutter as he lowered his forehead onto the bar and listened to his future coming towards him.

Oxford Makeover

JENNY BURRAGE

Shelley hummed to herself along with the hoover but it was the sort of hum that meant she had something on her mind. It wasn't tuneful. To the listener, if there had been one, it was horrible – a horrible duet between woman and machine. Edward was her problem and what to get her husband for his fiftieth birthday. A vision of him came to mind and that was horrible too.

What had happened to the handsome guy she had fallen for all those years ago? She looked at their wedding photo, still there on the wall after nearly twenty-five years. The one next to it showed him aged seventeen in swimming gear with his team from the swimming club. Was that really Eddie? She didn't think he could touch his toes any more, let alone see them. His hair was straggly and hung round his neck like grey spaghetti. His face had become red and podgy through too much alcohol and lack of exercise she supposed. Fifty was the new forty or something like that, wasn't it?

She looked at the clock. She'd have to leave for work in a minute and she hadn't decided on anything. A party? No, that meant asking all the relations and she couldn't face her mother-in-law fussing over Eddie as if he were still ten years old, and his much younger sister bringing her badly behaved kids along.

'Has he got any hobbies?' The girls at work were trying to help Shelley. He hadn't, unless you called it watching Sky Sports channels every evening until he went to bed.

'What about a balloon ride?' one suggested. He was afraid of heights, couldn't even go up a ladder.

Then… 'Why don't you book a romantic weekend away somewhere, Shelley?'

Of course. Why hadn't she thought of that before?

'Too late. I've booked it,' she told him firmly. 'I can't cancel it now. A weekend in Oxford where we met all those years ago. Lovely.'

'It's a white elephant,' he complained.

'What do you mean?'

'It's a bloody expensive present that I don't want. You like the idea of it, Shell, but it's my birthday and it's not my choice.'

She looked at him slouched in the chair, a picture of misery. He had no idea what else she had planned for him… fortunately.

'It's that famous hotel in Oxford, the Randolph. You know the one in the Inspector Morse series. It's got everything you could possibly desire, Eddie.'

'I wanted to watch the football,' he moaned.

'Sorry,' she said.

'Look, they've put the flags out for you Eddie,' Shelley said as they arrived at the hotel's entrance where the huge Union Jacks flapped above their heads. It's like they knew it was your birthday.' There was no reply, well maybe a grunt.

They sampled the Randolph's delicious celebration

afternoon tea in the Drawing Room when they arrived on Friday afternoon. No expense spared, naturally. Scones and clotted cream, dainty sandwiches, cakes and pastries, and a glass of champagne. Shelley toasted Eddie but he seemed oblivious to her efforts or to their surroundings, although the food disappeared remarkably quickly.

After tea they wandered into Magdalen Street and Shelley noticed the two-for-one suit offer in the clearance sale in Debenhams' window. How she persuaded Eddie to go in, she didn't know. Maybe it was the thought of her paying as part of the birthday package that did it.

'Pleased?' she asked as he came out carrying two bags.

'Nothing wrong with my old suit,' he grumbled. But there was, you could see your face in the seat of his trousers.

Shelley didn't tell him she'd booked an appointment in 'Toni & Guy' hair salon in George Street for Saturday morning or for a massage at the hotel in their spa room. She was beginning to wonder if this whole weekend had been a good idea.

Back at the Randolph she hoped that during the evening they would sip cocktails in the Morse Bar before they had dinner, but Eddie wanted a beer. Never mind, it was his birthday after all. She sighed. Things could only get better.

Afterwards they had dinner in the Acanthus restaurant. Shelley found some information on a sheet inside the menu before they chose their meal.

'Listen Eddie.' She read out,

'Where many other hotels, hotel chains and restaurants are de-skilling and buying ingredients pre-cooked or prepared from frozen, our chefs work from whole raw ingredients using only the finest and freshest produce. The beauty of the dish is the greatness of the ingredients with a focus on simplicity.'

'And look, there's more about suppliers and stuff like sustainable sources. Isn't that good?'

'I'm having the steak,' said Eddie and buried his head in the menu.

It was a memorable meal. Shelley chose salt roasted beetroot with goat's cheese cream to start, pan-seared cod with salted fennel & brown crab with pesto for main course and, to finish, salted caramel eclair. Eddie had soup of the day, steak and tarte tatin.

'Why don't they call it apple pie?' He liked good old plain cooking, did Eddie. He didn't like fancy names. Shelley wondered if she would ever convert him to trying new things.

After the cheese course, Eddie sat back, patted his stomach and burped loudly. He'd obviously enjoyed that part of the day.

'I'm ready for bed,' he said. Shelley almost felt this could be good news. Maybe he was feeling romantic after their time together in Oxford, ending with a wonderful meal. It wasn't to be. The four-poster bed was dreamy but it had to remain in Shelley's dreams as Eddie was snoring within two minutes of his head touching the pillow.

Next morning, after a hearty breakfast of bacon and egg and everything you could possibly imagine to go with it, Eddie had slunk off for his massage.

'I'm not up for this,' he told Shelley. 'I wanted a lie-in on my birthday weekend.' All the same he went off still muttering to himself. Shelley wished he hadn't been wearing a vest. Nobody of his age wore them anymore, did they? She blamed his mother.

'Good?' she asked him as he wandered back to their room.

'I nearly went to sleep,' he said.

His face reddened and she thought he was going to burst when she told him about the hair appointment.

'It's been booked at Toni & Guy, the famous hairdressing salon. Only the best for you on your birthday, Eddie.'

'What is this, an endurance test?' he spluttered. 'Can you cancel it?'

'It's in ten minutes and I've paid in advance,' she explained. 'It's just down George Street.'

The result was amazing. Surely this couldn't be Eddie, walking towards her.

'Wow! Turn round,' she said.

Reluctantly he did a little twirl. The back was shaped neatly to a point and the front was short and slightly spiked on top. It was a kind of russet colour now and shining with a healthy glow. The straggles had miraculously disappeared. He looked years younger.

'You look great,' she announced.

'It's not me,' he said, but all the same he kept looking at his reflection in the shop windows as they passed. She reckoned he was secretly pleased.

Sunday, their last day in Oxford, was not to be wasted. Shelley persuaded the new unrecognisable Eddie to go with her to the hotel's mini gym after breakfast for a work-out. She knew he wouldn't go by himself.

'It will do us both good,' she said.

Eddie ignored the weights and eventually settled for

the rowing machine, loudly puffing and panting as his arms thrust backwards and forwards. Shelley tried out the treadmill and the cycling machine. She felt suddenly fresher and vowed to visit her local gym more often and maybe Eddie would come too, but then again pigs might fly.

After all that exercise and a shower, they walked to the King's Arms where they'd met all those years ago. Shelley linked arms with Eddie but he didn't appear to notice, just ambled stolidly along as if she wasn't there.

They sat outside at the benches and tables at the front of the building to have their drinks. Shelley leaned across the table.

'Do you remember we sat here on that hot day drinking ice-cold beers and you asked me to go out with you?'

'No.' he said. 'Are you sure it was me?' She laughed. She knew he was joking. Or was he?

The girls at work couldn't wait to hear how the weekend went.

'Poor you,' they said.

'Ah,' she said,' but don't forget he's really fanciable now.'

'Lucky you!' they said.

That evening when Eddie came home from work, wearing one of his new suits and spiked up hair style, he was actually smiling, which was totally out of character. That birthday weekend had really been worth it. He was definitely different, purposeful. He didn't even switch on the TV.

'I've been promoted, Shell,' he told her. 'I'm the new warehouse manager. I applied for the job a few weeks ago. Never told you in case I didn't get it.'

'Great,' she said.

'More money.' He clapped his hands as if applauding himself and his good fortune.

'Great.'

'Yes it is and by the way I shall be away next weekend to do with the job.'

'Great,' she said again. 'Well done you!'

Eddie puffed out his cheeks.

'Yes, I've arranged a little bonding overnight stay at the Randolph for some of the staff. At our place all the ones who get new jobs have a chance to get to know each other better. Away from work, see. It's tradition and I liked the Randolph. Perfect for what I want.'

'Great.' Shelley hugged him. The birthday weekend had been a huge success. He was a different Eddie. 'How many of you are going?'

'Oh, only two this time. Me and that new young blonde girl who's going to be my secretary.'

The Macdonald Randolph Hotel is the leading 5-star hotel in Oxford. Built in 1864, it offers luxurious accommodation and award winning food and drink. It is famous for its appearance in the Inspector Morse TV series adapted from the novels by Colin Dexter.

Surveying Beaumont Street

NEIL HANCOX

Beaumont Street barely registered the young man setting up the tripod outside the Randolph Hotel. Tony Jenkins, in his Hi-Glow jacket and hard hat, sighted the laser theodolite along the street towards Worcester College. He tried to focus on the vertical target; figures interfered with his view; there was one attractive blonde head, then it disappeared; he pressed the button. No need to record any details in his notebook; everything was in the computer memory. How long, he wondered, would it be before he was superfluous, his place taken by a robot or a drone? One reading completed, another seven to go; perhaps he would spot that blonde head again?

He yawned and recalled last night in the pub; coffee was what he needed now. A group of tourists emerged from Gloucester Street, blocking the pavement while waiting for a gap in the traffic. Tony picked out the leader's umbrella and recorded the distance and direction. 'I must remember to delete that reading later,' he muttered; his BSc beckoned in eleven months, and his tutor was lacking in several qualities especially a sense of humour.

The woman was in her late twenties, Tony judged, bright red hair and a pale face, nice figure though and smart shoes. Should he call after her, say she had dropped something, ask her out for a drink tonight? His thoughts were too slow. Magda hardly noticed the young man adjusting some equipment and partially blocking the pavement; just another Oxford body among many. She was in a hurry, she was late.

'Overslept again?' the porter leered at her as she rushed through the staff entrance of the hotel.

Smile, she could not afford to lose this job. Her phone vibrated; it would be her boyfriend Tomazek or her mother, one wanting more money the other wondering when would she be home and could she bring… The pay here might be good compared with that in Poland but it cost a lot more to live. Tomazek, ever faithful? she doubted it. It was about time she ditched him. There would be threats and promises and her mother would be disappointed. She pulled her keys from her bag, unlocked her office and switched on the computer; now for the immediate problems of Oxford's largest and best hotel, The Randolph.

A couple started to cross the street from the Playhouse towards the Ashmolean Museum. A horn blared and a driver braked and swore. Tony Jenkins looked up from his phone and saw the man and woman continue unhurriedly across the road. Beaumont Street took this minor disturbance in its stride. It was used to feet, hooves, wheels and accidents; it tolerated road works, resurfacing and other indignities; it would outlast all the perpetrators. People and goods always had to get through.

Inside the entrance hall of the museum, the man read the notices while his wife pouted. 'What do we want to see all this old stuff for?' she asked.

'We are tourists, my dear, and that's what tourists do. Come on let's see the Greek and Roman sculptures, then we'll get a coffee.'

The coffee served in England was... ugh... Nothing like the real drink served in France. Her husband was striding out, not listening.

His wife shrugged; perhaps the wine in the Randolph tonight would be excellent. Meanwhile she must tolerate this man's strange ideas. She would no doubt learn more as their honeymoon progressed. Was that the right word?

Two hours later the French couple left the museum and re-crossed Beaumont Street, this time without incident. Tony Jenkins had moved to the junction of Walton Street with Beaumont Street and was standing with his back to Worcester College. He had refreshed himself with coffee and doughnuts in the nearby Playhouse Cafe, talked about football and arranged to go to a party that night; now it was time for a little more work. Beaumont Street, he thought, must be among the best surveyed parts of Oxford.

As he started to make another observation, he noted several heads and shoulders in his field of view, and a young woman surreptitiously drawing the last puff of nicotine from a cigarette. She stubbed the remains out on the pavement and wafted her hand across her open mouth a few times before extracting a spray from her pocket to fully restore sweet breath. Close by was a small, well polished, plaque advertising discrete dental services. She re-entered the building and resumed her position behind the enquiries desk together with the senior receptionist.

'You've been smoking Holly, haven't you?' the latter said. 'And I thought you had disappeared to get milk and coffee.'

The young woman coloured slightly. 'I was desperate. You know I gave up three weeks ago but in the club last night...'

her voice trailed off.

The receptionist shrugged. The wedding ring she wore hid a life of disappointment only made bearable by strict standards and, today, economies which enabled her to keep her small flat with its faded cat and curtains. There never had been a husband or partner. One had appeared on the horizon thirty-one years ago, nearly docked and then thought better of it. She had bought the dress in anticipation and still kept it in an old case. Unlike the young people today she had never bounced back. Secretly she didn't disapprove of them, she envied their energy and love of life.

The dentist's waiting room was not busy. Holly, her poise now recovered, was gazing out of the window. 'Look, there's a crowd of children over there,' she pointed, 'coming out of Walton Street and turning up towards the big museum.' Her companion smiled at the description of the Ashmolean.

A crocodile of nine, ten and eleven year olds, in pairs and marshalled by teachers, swirled past Tony Jenkins; an educational outing, no doubt judged useful by someone, somewhere, he surmised. As the children rounded the corner into Beaumont Street two girls, hand in hand, saw the blue plaque.

'What's that?' one of them asked.

It would be Marjorie with the question the teacher knew. Always asking but not always listening.

'It says that Kings Richard I and John were born in a house there 800 years ago.' The teacher pointed to a large patch of brambles and small trees.

'I don't see a house,' Marjorie retorted.

'That's because they lived a very long time ago.'

'Do we get a burger for lunch, Miss?' the two girls asked,

having lost interest in kings and queens, adding quickly, 'with chips.'

A young teaching assistant heard their plea. She wished she could reassure her charges but feared that it might not be a healthy option, which was compulsory.

Unknown to the procession of young minds, in one of the Georgian buildings they were passing, an emeritus professor and one of his students were sifting through a pile of competition entries.

The academic waved one at his accomplice. 'You passed this,' he said accusingly. 'Absolute crap, breaks every rule in the short story canon; too many characters, no conflict, no resolution…' The student, mature and confident, had no intention of being bullied. She knew this tirade would soon peter out and normal relations be resumed.

'What you fail to understand,' she said, 'is that stories are artificial constructs showing life as a tidy sequence; of character, conflict and resolution. In reality life is messy, unsatisfying and often unfair; we catch glimpses of it, misinterpret what we see and then it's past. We adopt the literary fiction in order to make our existence bearable.' She was not sure that she believed all this but it quietened her adversary.

He puffed and smiled. 'You are clearly one of my students,' he said, as he reluctantly restored the manuscript to the 'possible' pile, adding 'how about a stroll up Beaumont Street culminating with a drink at the Randolph?'

'You're on, let's go,' the woman replied, though she knew that when it came to pay he would have forgotten his wallet and she would have to find her purse.

The academic, instantly recognisable by his long hair

and the plastic bag clutched in one hand, accompanied by a smart young woman, emerged from the doorway of the Georgian building and started to walk along the pavement, blocking Tony Jenkins' view for what seemed an eternity to the impatient young man. Why didn't people walk more quickly? One last reading and he was off for the day.

As he folded up his tripod and was about to hoist it over his shoulder, she appeared, the red-haired woman from the Randolph. She was in an even greater hurry, with a sheaf of papers under one arm and her eyes on her phone. It was probably an uneven paving stone; she tripped and pitched forward. This time Tony Jenkins was ready.

'Are you all right?' he asked as he broke her fall; her scent was pleasant.

Magda caught her breath, hesitated, 'Yes, thank you.'

He steadied her for another second or so. Her body relaxed. 'I'm going to a party tonight in St Clements,' he said, 'would you like to come? I could pick you up from the Randolph at 8.00 tonight...'

Thoughts were racing round her head; she was in a hurry; she was dropping her moaning boyfriend back home; why not take up this offer? She studied the open face: no tattoos, clean shaven, blue eyes. 'OK, I'll see you later on,' she replied.

Beaumont Street smiled. It made a change to bring two young people together – perhaps it should try to do that more often and ignore the occasional traffic jam. It was more fun.

Whatever it Takes

JACKIE VICKERS

Harriet snatched the letter from the tray on the hall table, hid it in her pocket and ran upstairs to her room. She locked the door and leant against it, tearing at the envelope with her thumb nail, for she had recognised her Aunt Louisa's writing and did not wish to have to explain the contents to her mother.

Dorothy Winter, Harriet's mother, had made it plain she was embarrassed by her sister.

'Outrageous behaviour! She has brought dishonour to this family,' she had sobbed on hearing the news. 'All the servants will be laughing behind my back.'

'We only have three,' Harriet pointed out, 'Cook, Ellen and Old John.'

'Servants talk, Harriet, that is the point. Soon all our neighbours will know, just about the whole of Summertown.'

Harriet nodded gravely. 'The whole of Oxford, even.'

Mrs Winter gave her a sharp look, but her daughter was bent over her sketch book, frowning slightly.

'Some of my friends think she is wonderful, being so active for The Cause,' she said quietly.

'But you and your friends are very young, dear. You don't always understand that actions can have consequences.'

'Do you think Aunt Louisa understood what the consequences would be of chaining herself to those railings, Mother?'

Dorothy Winter's eyes bulged with the effort of restraining herself, for Ellen had announced that lunch was served, and the less a parlour-maid heard the better.

'Hush dear,' was all she said. 'Think of your poor father.'

But Francis Winter just threw his head back and laughed. 'It won't have hurt her to see the inside of a police station for a few hours.'

The Winter family lived in the leafy suburb of North Oxford. Many of their neighbours professed to liberal values; some of the young women had even adopted the New Woman fashions. But Mr and Mrs Francis Winter were distrustful of advanced ideas and hoped their eldest daughter would not be influenced by progressive views. With this in mind, they were careful to make friends among those who shared their opinions and interests. They were, however, kind people who tried hard to live up to certain standards of tolerance and understanding. As Francis Winter was fond of declaring: 'tolerance oils the wheels of society', though Dorothy Winter sometimes found difficulty putting this into practice, particularly where her servants were concerned.

'I do try and see things from their point-of-view and make allowances, limited education and so on, but how difficult can it be to make a pudding? Any pudding? The Hetheringtons' cook manages perfectly well. And we never have more than eight guests...' Harriet's mother took every opportunity to point out the limitations of their dining room, for in the larger houses down Banbury Road it was perfectly possible to seat a dozen guests. A larger social circle would be beneficial to Harriet and her sisters and increase their chances, for their girls' future was never far from her thoughts. Harriet's best friend had gained admission to Somerville College to study mathematics, which did not seem a very feminine activity and was troubling news. Fortunately Harriet preferred drawing which, she has been reassured, is still a perfectly acceptable leisure occupation.

'Think what some mothers have to face,' Mrs Winter's friend reminded her, 'Mrs Hetherington's daughter went on a Suffragette March in Trafalgar Square. She is only twenty-one, but they have so much liberty nowadays.'

Dorothy Winter felt not a little complacent at this news. Harriet has so far proved quite docile, so long as she is allowed the freedom to draw and paint, and though she has spent more time with her Aunt Louisa than either parent would like, she has never hankered for mathematics or taken clandestine trips to London.

While her mother judiciously considered her every move in the drawing rooms of North Oxford, Harriet took long walks through the parks, sketch book at the ready. Regular exercise kept her headaches at bay and had been recommended by her doctor who understood the frustrations of a young person forced into inactivity.

'Nothing that fresh air and long walks won't put right,' he said, nodding as though in deep thought. Dorothy Winter left reassured, not seeing him smile at her daughter with complicity.

In the two years since she left school, Harriet had contrived to extend her personal space. She sketched when her mother was out and disappeared well before any lunches or tea-parties took place. She was careful to maintain a calm and friendly manner towards everyone, but slipped away before anyone could make demands on her time. 'Such a delightful girl,' they said. Nevertheless, despite this relative freedom, Harriet was beginning to feel her life had become intolerable.

Three years have passed since that memorable occasion when an eminent artist came to dine. The Winters proudly showed off their daughter's sketch books but were astounded and not a little dismayed at his response.

'This talent' he cried, energetically waving one of the sketchbooks, 'must be nurtured!' He repeatedly emphasised Harriet's ability and insisted something should be done about it, explaining that a growing number of young ladies now attended Art Schools. Her parents were a little shaken by this unwelcome news, and did not invite him again. They were convinced that art in any form should be no more than a pleasant pastime for a lady. Harriet pleaded, raged and sulked, but they were unyielding, even though the Ruskin School of Drawing was only a short walk away.

Aunt Louisa's little escapade, as Harriet's father called it, did have serious consequences. There was the matter of several broken windows in Regent Street, for Louisa and her fellow Suffragettes had concealed bricks under their coats. Abusive language was also claimed to have been heard. These ladies had all been sentenced to several weeks in Holloway Prison, and Harriet soon wrote to her aunt to express her admiration, but also to ask her advice. The years were passing and she felt no nearer to studying at the Ruskin, or anywhere else.

When Louisa's reply arrives, Harriet is disappointed. It is a long letter all about fighting for justice and for women's rights and only at the end does she refer to her niece's concerns,

'So, dear Harriet, I urge you to do whatever it takes to achieve your goal.'

Harriet crumples the letter and throws herself on the bed, both angry and disappointed. She lies there thinking for a while, then sits up and smoothes out the letter carefully and re-reads it. This time she reads the words 'do whatever it takes' as a call for action. 'Thank you Aunt Louisa', she whispers.

Harriet knows all about the Ruskin School. She is familiar with the Ashmolean Galleries, for she spends most mornings there drawing some exhibit, or making a careful study of a painting. The school is on the top floor but Harriet has ventured no further than the bottom step of the stairs to the upper galleries, always vanishing when students appear. Her mother imagines she is walking around the shops, examining the latest fashions on display or exchanging secrets with a friend as they walk in the University Parks. Today, Harriet stands by the stairs to the School of Drawing on the upper galleries and dreams for a while. She watches the students come and go then turns round and quickly walks over to their notice board. She has an idea.

A few days later, Harriet is standing in the deep shadow cast by the museum portico. She has rolled up her fashionably long, navy jacket and removed her hat. She pulls a tight bundle from her capacious bag and shakes out the shabby coat and hat she has taken from their servant's room. Ellen will not have noticed their absence as she will be busy helping Cook with preparations for tonight's dinner party. Harriet puts the coat on and frowns in discomfort at the coarse fabric of the ill-fitting garment, then pulls the hat firmly down over her thick hair. She walks through the main entrance, head bent, avoiding eye-contact with museum staff who may recognise her. Usually she runs lightly up the stairs to the first floor galleries, eager to begin her work. Today her feet are heavy, her leg muscles unresponsive. A wave of resentment washes through her. Why should she have to go through such humiliation for what is surely her right? Her father has always insisted on the importance of education, even for girls. 'But only if it does not interfere with their chances of making a good marriage,' she mutters. And how often does that happen? To give herself courage, Harriet repeats her aunt's words to herself, 'whatever it takes, whatever it takes'. A young man with a shock of red hair, carrying a large folder, smiles and asks if he can help. Harriet explains that she has an appointment with Professor Rothermere. He then takes her upstairs and leads her to a room where a tall, bearded man is bent over some drawings on a large table. The man waves her towards a folding screen which stands by a large sofa, covered with a white sheet.

'Take your clothes off,' he says, barely looking at her.

Harriet places her sketch book on the table in front of him and goes to undress. She is shaking and has difficulty undoing all her buttons and hooks. Looking through a crack in the screen she sees that the man has picked up her book and is examining the drawings, taking them to the tall windows for a closer look. Harriet has now removed all her clothes and is taking deep breaths to control her shivering.

She pulls the pins from her hair, which tumbles over her back and shoulders, a thick mass of golden curls. Then she moves to the sofa and sits down, covering herself with her arms.

He turns and frowns a little.

'You're a little on the thin side,' he remarks, and leans forward to gently lift her arm along the curved back. Then he tells her to lie down, and adjusts her legs.

'You'll have to stop trembling and loosen up a bit if you come to work here.' His voice is stern, but Harriet notices a faint smile about his mouth.

'You've done this before?'

'No,' Harriet whispers.

'Perhaps some sitting for night-school students?'

She shakes her head.

The professor sits down on the sofa and strokes her foot. Then, pursing his lips, he half-closes his eyes and lifts her hair away from her shoulders. Then he slowly runs his fingers down her body, pausing now and again, making her gasp a little.

'A complete novice,' he says to himself, 'how very satisfactory.'

Harriet has closed her eyes, she cannot meet his penetrating gaze. She has found his touch unexpectedly pleasurable and she thinks he may have noticed.

After she has dressed he waves the sketch book at her.

'Where did you find this?' he shows her the cover with her name, Harriet Winter, 35 Bardwell Road, across the top in bold black letters. 'I am going there to dinner tonight,' he adds, looking confused.

'I know,' she replies. 'I am Harriet Winter.'

A look of horror passes across his face. She watches him as he drops into an armchair and rests his head in his hands. When he finally looks up, she sees the parts of his face not covered by beard are now a greenish-white and beaded with sweat.

'Did anyone see you come in here?'

'Quite a few,' Harriet says. 'A red-haired student showed me to your room; I should know him anywhere.'

Professor Rothermere struggles out of his chair and paces up and down, looking at the floor.

His collapse gives Harriet confidence, and she says ruthlessly, 'you haven't asked me why I am here.'

'To put me in a compromising position, I suppose.' She hears the bitterness in his voice.

Harriet ignores this and says in the gentle, educated tones of north Oxford,

'I should be very grateful if you would take me on as a student, here at the Ruskin.'

The professor looks at her, surprised.

'But there would be no difficulty, your drawings indicate remarkable talent,' and he starts flicking through her drawings to stop the tremor in his hands.

'My parents refuse to allow it,' Harriet says in a hard voice.

He frowns, not understanding.

'This can easily be resolved without anyone knowing.' Harriet nods towards the sofa, to be sure he understands.

'Tonight I shall have a migraine, so be reassured, I shall not be present at dinner. May I look forward to receiving an offer of a place at the Ruskin?'

'But if your parents disapprove...' he says helplessly.

Harriet looks at him. She has gained the upper hand and

is not about to lose her advantage. She moves towards the door.

'It is now in your hands, Professor Rothermere. *You must do whatever it takes.*'

Harriet Winter's paintings were much sought after in the inter-war years and are now mostly held in private collections. She lived for many years in a small house in Jericho which had an attic studio lit by skylights. Her young students recalled a Rothermere hanging there, a gift from the artist. It was called Reclining nude reading a letter.

The Ruskin School of Drawing and Fine Art was founded in 1871 by John Ruskin and stayed in the Ashmolean Galleries until 1974 when it moved to its current premises at 74 High Street. The museum galleries have recently been remodelled and display, among other things, a fine collection of paintings. Unfortunately the Ashmolean has not yet purchased any works by Rothermere or Winter.

Wilful Obstruction

H G EBNER

Oxford, 2052

Marjorie Boyle should have seen this coming. It was only a matter of time.

The dreaded letter arrived on Wednesday afternoon, officially 'inviting' Marjorie to attend an interview – for the role she already held. *Here we go again.*

As the longest serving staff member of the County Council's Work Automation and Realignment programme, rising from lowly assistant to Senior Realignment Coordinator in thirty-two years, she had outlasted more 'comprehensive reviews' than she could count. She was a survivor.

'*How do you do it?*' former colleagues asked with clucks of admiration and a pinch of jealousy. Marjorie's eternally cheerful disposition and non-threatening nature seemed to make her bullet-proof when it came to redundancy. Amiable neutrality, that was her hallmark. *Never let a twinge of frustration register on your face.*

And it helped that she didn't 'stand out'. Brown hair, brown eyes, a little overweight but certainly not fat, she had a round, unnoticeable face that rarely saw make-up. She rather blended into the background. Indispensable people were dispensed with all the time. But not Marjorie, she was the comfortable armchair of the office, a reliable piece of furniture that no one, not even senior leadership, was in any great hurry to part with. Frankly, she made their job so much easier. Keep smiling and uncomplainingly accept piles of additional work – that was her motto.

There was no level of aggravation that she couldn't tamp down with a good old-fashioned cake binge and a few glasses of Chardonnay. It was amazing what chocolate did to soothe her nerves. Not that it did anything good to her figure. All stirrings of moral outrage drowned in a light, chocolate-y inebriation. By morning, she could always face the day – and the absurdly impossible workload – with a smile.

Most people wouldn't want Marjorie's job in the first place. The Work Automation and Realignment Programme, fittingly known as WARP, was viewed with deep misgiving by anyone who still had a job in Oxford. In 2052, there were precious few left. Cashier-less tills, driver-less cars, and doctor-less surgeries – not quite as wonderful as advertised. Not, that is, for cashiers, taxi drivers and doctors. If you received a letter from the WARP office, it wasn't good news. A referral to meet with Marjorie or her colleagues could only mean one thing: your job had been replaced by a robot. Not a sci-fi sort of robot, mind you. Realignment Coordinators were at pains to clarify: *'No actual robots will be doing your job, Mr Smith; it has simply been automated!'*

As if that helped.

Telling a postal clerk two years shy of retirement with full pension that he's been replaced by a U-Mail-It! machine is a demoralizing blow, no matter how you present it.

'Mr Smith,' all the Realignment Specialists were trained to say, *'this is a chance to re-align your skills with the changing*

workplace.' Changing? It was simply disappearing.

Marjorie never used that line. It grated on people's nerves. She preferred to go off-script; to put her heart and soul into relaying the bad news with genuine optimism.

'What have you always wished you had more time for? Have you ever wanted to travel? Start a business? Learn to play guitar?'

Whatever the thing was they'd dreamed of, Marjorie had a knack for finding it – the silver lining in a 'realignment' – one that rang true. She helped hairdressers become gardeners, IT specialists become song-writers, dental hygienists, become designers and cashiers become athletes and bicycle repairmen.

It wasn't easy. Some people lost their job more than once. They honed a new skill, only to find it, too, on the chopping block of automation. The ever-shrinking world of work was confounding but Marjorie had the patience of a saint. That's why they gave her the hard cases. She listened as they railed against the system but she never took it personally. And the thing was, they could see she really cared. Nine hundred and eighty six of them had friended her on Lifebook – now that was saying something.

Of course, her style didn't win over everyone but it certainly kept violent outbursts of indignation to a minimum. Marjorie held the county-wide record for 'fewest abusive re-alignment incidents'. Just two and one of them hardly counted, it was her husband. Ex-husband. Telling a man who'd driven lorries all his life that a 'person' was no longer required behind the wheel was met with fiery expletives and the launch of a stapler and other desk paraphernalia out of the window onto the street below. Perhaps Marjorie's suggestion that he could finally fix up the old shed he'd been complaining about, was ill-judged. But frankly, it was a little unfair to make Marjorie handle the re-alignment on that occasion, even if she was in charge of 'hard cases'. She could have refused but Marjorie always did what was asked of her, regardless of how unfair or ridiculous the County's request might be. Say what you like, she might be divorced but she still had a job (which was more than she could say for Dave).

She unfolded the letter and read it again.

Clearly written by someone out of touch with reality it enthused, 'This is an exciting time…' *Really? For whom exactly?* 'Advances in technology have offered us an unprecedented opportunity to improve efficiency and reduce workplace stress...' *Improve efficiency?* She'd heard that before. Once again, Marjorie would compete for a dwindling number of jobs, along with the rest of the team.

Except, there was no more team.

Marjorie was not only the *longest* serving staff member, she was now the *only* staff member – unless you counted her supervisor, Bill. And technically, he was part of senior leadership. The team had been engaged in an endless game of musical chairs but, the last time the music stopped, there was only one chair left. And Marjorie was sitting in it.

'Sorry to bother you. I think I must have missed something,' Marjorie said to her supervisor late that afternoon. 'Who else will be interviewed for my role? I think I'm the only one left…'

Bill did not want to say. He rocked back on his heels a little uncomfortably and sucked air through his teeth. 'No one else will be interviewed but you Marjorie. And uh…

well, one other, you know, 'non-person.'

Of course.

Non-person was the accepted euphemism for 'robot', a term to be avoided at all costs as it tended to spark negative headlines. MPs had learned the hard way that the papers would have an absolute field-day with any news of local councils employing robots instead of real people. The press went so far as to report that the Conservative Party was exploring a possible legal framework to grant non-persons ('robots') the right to vote – since so many of them were actively employed and, the article ominously warned, they were probably programmed to vote Conservative. How could anyone be sure? While the allegations were staunchly denied, any reference to 'robots' was quietly banned by anyone in government.

Marjorie's eyes were wide open in disbelief. She opened her mouth and an intake of breath signalled she had something to say. But years of experience trained her to close it. She pressed her lips together and silently counted to ten. She smiled, slowly – it looked painful.

So that was it.

Marjorie's job itself was slated for automation. Until now, most realignment work had been protected. Someone with a shred of common sense and decency had appreciated that meeting with people made redundant by robots should probably be done by 'people'. Anything else would be in bad taste. Apparently, even common sense is vulnerable to budget cuts.

Bill tried to help, rambling on, 'Preposterous idea, isn't it. Having a robot talk to people who've just been sacked by robots? Our abusive incident numbers will go through the roof!' He stifled an awkward laugh.

Marjorie's face was smiling but it lacked a certain authenticity, as if she was merely squinting.

He continued, 'Did I say robots? I meant non-persons. Anyway, don't give this another thought, Marjorie. Just do what you've been doing all these years. It'll be fine.'

Bill knew perfectly well his assurances were misplaced – touching, but misplaced. And in all their years working together, Marjorie had never known him to try to crack a joke.

She trudged along the corridor. A once beautiful building was now mostly empty. With most of her colleagues gone, the offices next to hers now housed shelves of blinking computer servers. The County Council headquarters rented office space in what was once the Ashmolean Museum. Wandering around an *actual* museum had become the sort of pastime only grannies and academics engaged in. Once the entire collection had been digitized, and it was accessible by anyone, anywhere, at any time, the objects themselves became well, redundant. Guess the Director didn't see that coming. *It would have been fine*, he bitterly quipped in the paper, *if not for those damned Holoview Tours*. Who could have anticipated their runaway success? Artefacts in amazing holographic detail and historical settings beamed onto surrounding walls could transform anyone's living room into ancient Rome or the Shrine of King Taharqa. Why leave home? The Museum now rented out the building.

Even the old canteen was no longer staffed by 'persons'. VLAD the Vegan Lunch-A-Matic Dispenser, housed behind a thick glass enclosure, was a giant vending machine. No smiles and banter offered with your bacon bap. Just VLAD's synthetic Russian voice and robotic arm dispensing warm tea, weak coffee and limp cress sandwiches.

Marjorie stared glumly out of the window of her office. She watched the traffic on Beaumont Street below. Self-driving pods moved seamlessly, equally spaced, efficiently carrying passengers along the current of a steady flowing stream. Watching them numbed the mind. Perfect. Predictable. Boring. She missed the sound of beeping horns, the bubbly liveliness of an honest city street. Like a freshly opened can of soda pop, the streets used to tickle her senses. She sighed deeply, sorry for the lifeless road below. It looked more like a conveyor belt than a street.

The Council had really let their standards slip. Formal letters were being scrapped 'to save trees'. Interviews with realignment coordinators were being scrapped 'to save dignity'. These days, most people out of a job were sent a 100-character text with a link to the County's joblist and a voucher for one hour's 'Decompression Therapy' at Worcester College Yoga & Wellness Retreat. The only thing keeping Marjorie employed was all the 'hard cases'. No amount of algorithmic programming had (up until now) been able to cope with the unpredictable array of human responses to being-made-redundant-by-a-robot. The criers, arguers, disbelievers, negotiators, and possible plotters – they were Marjorie's charges. And she worked long hours to deliver realignment services and, importantly to her, help change a few lives.

But not anymore.

Come Friday, it seemed that she too might well be out of a job.

Marjorie abstained from her usual half bottle of Chardonnay the night before her interview. She ironed the nicest (or least frumpy) dress she could still fit into and went to bed early. Friday morning, the sky was bright and sunny as she left her semi-detached house. It would all be OK. She was a survivor, wasn't she? She swiped her mobile watch and, within minutes, a driverless pod-car pulled up outside her house. She stepped into the pod, as a series of voice prompts requested her GPS destination. She chose an innocuous radio station and hummed cheerfully along. Attitude was everything on a day like this. But as her pod reached the first roundabout thick grey clouds were starting to roll in, and by the time she reached her stop outside the County Council building, it had started to chuck it down.

Gloomy weather reflected just the sort of mood that would grip most people in her circumstances. But not Marjorie. She rallied every fibre of her being to maintain the amiable disposition that had stood her in good stead all these years. She stepped out of the pod and scrambled toward the building, not bothering to open her brolly. As she reached the top step, she heard the loud, staccato sound of the pod-car's personal protection system hailing her. *Wait. (pause) Wait. (pause) You–have–for-got-ten some-thing.*

She patted herself down. Purse, brolly, mobile watch – all present. What could the stupid pod be bleating about? She ducked back through the cold rain, into the waiting car, scanning the floor and running her hands along the back seat. A-ha! Her earring. Marjorie was loathe to admit it, but this was a rather ingenious feature. Driverless pod-cars could not resume travel to their next destination if any personal object had been left inside the vehicle, particularly if it had a telltale whiff of DNA. This wasn't an original design feature – more of a response to catastrophic legal suits. A six-figure case, involving a paraplegic's trainer foot whisked around town for hours by a pod-car with an overly hasty departure and a missed Olympic dream, persuaded companies that such a safety feature might be a good idea. Now reprogrammed, pod-cars would not budge, continuing to hail the occupants until their forgotten item was retrieved.

Marjorie put the earring back on and dashed up the steps once again, through the columned entrance into the County Council building. Taking the lift to the second floor, she checked her face in the mirrored panel, making sure it displayed an air of cheerful indifference. *Breezy, unflustered amiability* – that was the thing to aim for.

'Thanks for being such a good sport Marjorie.' Bill gave her hand a conciliatory squeeze. He gestured toward the room in which the interview panel was waiting. 'Good luck.'

'Thanks Bill,' Marjorie smiled. 'Not worried. It's the robot who needs luck,' she chirped.

'Let's hope so,' he mumbled unheard.

It was quite possibly – no, very definitely – the most humiliating experience of her life. Inviting someone to interview for the job they have successfully done for more than 30 years, whilst a robotic doppelganger is being interviewed for the same job, was a new low, even for the County Council. Competing against colleagues was always unpleasant enough but competing against an inanimate object? Marjorie now deeply understood how the people she'd helped realign over the years must have felt. It really stung.

When it was over, she smiled graciously and somehow managed to sound genuine as she thanked the interviewers for '*giving me the opportunity*'. She was led into her supervisor's office to wait for news while the panel deliberated.

Marjorie could not think. All she could hear was the irritating click of Bill's clock. She had never noticed it before, there on the wall above his desk. Now its incessant click, click, click was like a time bomb counting seconds to certain destruction. She swiped at her mobile watch and flicked through Lifebook updates. The dental hygienist just got remarried. A former postal worker just published his book. Her favourite bus driver, the one who ranted for nearly an hour, had posted a picture of his zipwire freefall in Costa Rica. A few others had posted marathon race times, recipes and pictures of their pets. Marjorie 'liked' them all. They made her last 30 years of work seem worthwhile.

Finally, Bill opened the door. The look on his face was not encouraging.

'Sorry to keep you waiting, Ms Boyd.'

Ms Boyd? That's formal. What happened to Marjorie?

'I don't know how to tell you this but,' he puffed his cheeks and blew air out the sides. 'I'm afraid they decided to give the job to a non-person.'

Keep the face even. Be amiable.

Marjorie cleared her throat. 'When you say 'the' job, do you mean 'my' job?' she asked as brightly and non-threateningly as possible. *Adopt an air of mere clarification.* 'I was sure the letter mentioned a consultation process. And I would just like to reassure the Council that I'd be happy to help the Realignment Team in any capacity you see fit. I mean, 42 re-alignments a week now, some of them really tough cases. And I know you have budget cuts, Bill. I completely appreciate that. So, I just want to say that I'd be very happy to take reduced pay and work longer hours to, you know, get us over the big hurdle. Just trying to be helpful...' she continued.

'Please, don't make this any harder for me, Marj.' Bill looked dismayed but resolute.

'Sorry – gosh no! Of course not,' she giggled awkwardly at herself. 'I wouldn't dream of that. You know me Bill. Never one to be a bother,' she paused. 'But maybe just one quick query? I feel like I must have misread or misheard or misunder...'

'Look, you didn't misunderstand Marj. They've decided they can meet the needs of re-alignment services in the Council fully with a single non-person.'

'Oh,' she replied still processing. No trace of emotion in the voice or face – yet. *Stay calm.* 'I see. Understood. No worries, Bill.'

Silence hung.

'May I just ask,' she began brightly, a little *too* brightly, 'where I let myself down? Sorry, where I let 'persons' down? In the interview, I mean. Is there any constructive feedback the panel wished to share with me?'

Bill examined her face intently, scanned her body language looking for signs of a crack in the façade. He had the expression of a man who desperately required the loo, a nervous casting about of the eyes, searching for appropriately polite excuses that would allow him to escape from the present situation post haste. 'Marj, you've been an admirable asset to...'

'So, no feedback then?' she chirped loudly,

uncharacteristically interrupting him. 'I really do want to learn for the sake of self-improvement exactly how a robot – sorry, a *non-person* – can be better at this job than *me* – sorry, better than *a person*.'

Bill began to respond; his mouth partially opened but he thought better of it, and Marjorie had already jumped in.

'Go on, Bill. What does it say in your report there? Hmm? I have given exemplary service for over thirty years and always with a smile, Bill. Always with a smile. I've been doing the work of twelve people – twelve!' her voice was increasing in volume, 'and I never complained. Not once. In thirty years. I let people go all the time, Bill. People with families, with bills to pay. I've seen lives ruined for what? To save a few quid, employing robots to do their jobs. But I have *always* given them something. Something to hang their hat on – to understand the absurdity of what is happening, to keep them from going insane, something to tell their mates down at the pub. So what is it Bill? Give me something. Anything. What did the robot do better? Where did I fall down? Was it recall of current employment legislation? What was I lacking?!!'

Bill quickly fumbled with the file. He raised one eyebrow as if warning – she wasn't going to like this. 'OK,' he said and read directly from the interview report. 'Personality.'

'What?!' Marjorie scrunched up her face.

'Personality,' he repeated in mild disbelief.

'The panel thinks I don't have enough personality?'

'No, no – too much of it, apparently.' He shrugged, attempting a gesture of solidarity.

'I'm losing my job to a robot because I have too much personality?' Marjorie asked, incredulous. Her neck was acquiring splotchy patches of red – they were creeping steadily up toward her cheeks. Without meaning to rise, she now found herself standing.

Bill did not enjoy this sort of conversation. He had problems of his own – namely a very tenuous grasp on his job as supervisor and a shopaholic wife blithely unaware of their overdraft limit. 'Look, don't take it personally, Marj. We all make sacrifices for modern life. Best thing to do is think of this as an opportunity, right? Dust off your CV and reinvigorate your working life or whatever it is you Realignment Coordinators always say. Or you could always get a cat?'

Marjorie didn't hear him. She had gathered her things and was half way down the hall, bustling toward the lift. She mashed the ground floor button hard. For more than thirty years she had put up with a lot – but she really had had enough.

As Marjorie crossed Beaumont Street, she had no clear destination in mind, but she certainly wasn't ready to go home. She was in desperate need of wine and a slice (or two) of chocolate cake. Heading toward Gloucester Green, she decided to try Wakeaccino's. It was one of those retro places, serving little cakes and lattes just like the ubiquitous coffee shops of the early 2000's. It was a little down at heel but they still had real people working there which gave it, in Marj's opinion, a nicer ambience. You had to overlook the fact that the 'baristas' only smiled and keyed in orders; they didn't really foam the milk for your cappuccino anymore. That was done behind the counter by 'caff-bots', cranking out mediocre froth for every cup. No waste. No mistakes. *When did uniformity get confused with perfection?* She ordered a large slice of Black Forest gâteau and builders' tea. Too early in the day for wine – even for Marjorie.

She flumped into a bench seat at the back of the café and glanced round at the half empty place. Until ten minutes earlier, Marjorie really had believed she would emerge from the interview with her job. Sure, she figured it would have come with worsened terms – longer hours, more cases, fewer days annual leave – but she never thought they'd be daft enough to hire a robot for *her* job. When was this absurdity going to end? She swiped a plump finger across the smart-screen table top, flicking through channels as she waited, but her mind was somewhere else.

'Black Forest gâteau?' called out a slender middle-aged woman with a very tidy black fringe. Marjorie raised her hand to claim it. She recognized the waitress – her former GP. If she blanked Marjorie completely, then she probably did not wish to be 'recognised' by former patients. But the woman held her gaze and smiled warmly, 'Here you are, Marjorie.' She set the slice of cake down on the table.

'Thanks, Dr Moore. What are you doing here? I thought you were still fighting the NHS over the big redundancy case?'

'Oh that,' the GP-turned-waitress said with a sly grin, 'still winding its way through the courts. I'm wearing them down. In the meantime, I took some good advice. You know, I finally realised that what I missed most wasn't the work exactly – it was the people. Well that, and having a reason to get up every morning. So, I've been working my way through a bunch of jobs, the few that still require human contact. It's been good fun. Anyway, when I'm finished, maybe I'll write a book about it.'

Marjorie understood. Talking to people was the thing

that she too loved most about her job. Even the hard cases. (Well, maybe not Dave.) She beamed her cheery Marjorie smile. 'Sounds like you got great advice. You must have a brilliant solicitor.'

Dr Moore cocked her head to one side and grinned, 'It was *your* advice, Marj. Too humble to take the compliment, I get it,' she winked, 'Well, enjoy your cake.'

She turned to leave but stopped in her tracks, her eyes caught by a BBC newsfeed playing on Marjorie's table-top screen. 'Bastard,' she said in voice that lowered the temperature of the room a few degrees. 'I'd love to see him get his due,' she shook her head in disgust. 'Anyway, lovely to see you, Marj. Keep up the good work!' and off she hurried to serve another customer.

Marjorie hadn't the heart to confess there was no longer any work for her to do. She looked down at the newsfeed still playing to see the object of her former GP's disdain: Bruns Vanderson, Chief Exec of Robotitech.

'*A staggering £1.5 billion pounds in profit announced today by the industry giant who put automation at the heart of the British economy. Bruns Vanderson unveiled his latest prototype, the SSS (Self-Sailing Ship), a captain-less freighter that promises greater efficiency...*'

Vanderson's manicured beard and slightly maniacal, blue eyes exuded counterfeit charm as he languidly spoke to reporters from the deck of his super yacht.

The penny dropped.

For thirty-two years, Marjorie had uncomplainingly helped people in Oxford, trying to make the best one could out of unfortunate situations. But for the first time, it occurred to her that she had unwittingly helped someone else. Someone who didn't deserve it. And she was not happy about that. Not at all.

A bolt of fury struck her with a mischievous thought. Before a single mouthful of chocolate cake could lull her into submission, she acted on impulse. She stormed out the door, marching toward Beaumont Street with determination, calling for a pod-car with her mobile watch as she went. There was one waiting for her outside the steps of the County Council, just as she reached the building. She faced the pod-car. All her frustration distilled in that scowl, she poured her contempt like lighter fluid onto the robot in front of her. Marjorie flung open the passenger door, removed the back of her earring and buried it deep down in between the back seat cushions. Then she spun on her heel and left the pod helplessly stuck there, moaning its electronic nonsense: *Wait. (pause) Wait. (pause) You-have-for-got-ten-some-thing.*

Over and over and over.

It wasn't much, just a little act of defiance but it felt good. It would cause a bit of a mess. Disrupt the perfect flow of traffic. Eventually, they'd have to send someone from the company to investigate the problem, check for the item, reset the pod-car and certify they'd done all this to avoid legal action. Meanwhile it would cause delay; no one else would get their pod-car on time. She felt a little better. Two fingers up to robots.

Marjorie headed home with three bottles of wine and three seasons of Poldark, an old favourite from her teens, to watch back-to-back. Apparently, she also posted a message to her 986 friends on Lifebook – sometime before season three and after bottle one of the Chardonnay.

```
'Replaced by robot. Not going down
without a gifht!'
```

And at some point, well after bottle two, she also posted a rather disjointed call to arms: everyone should leave something in their pod-cars and create a traffic jam of apocalyptic proportions in front of County Council headquarters – *take a stand!* She also sent round a few defaced images of Bruns Vanderson, first with devil's horns, then with a distorted robot head lounging on the deck of the SSS Loser.

Saturday morning, Marjorie awoke to a thumping headache and a surprising turn of events. Eloquence, it seemed, was not necessary when you hit a nerve. Regardless of how rambling and barmy her ideas might have been, Marjorie clearly lit a spark. Hundreds of friends and contacts understood exactly how she felt and had replied to her posts. The outpouring of support was comforting. But as she sipped a glass of water and popped a few paracetamol, she had the nagging feeling that she might have acted rashly. With a pounding head and cotton-wool mouth, she went into town. The unpleasant task of collecting personal items from her office awaited.

If she'd ever doubted the genuineness of affection from those she'd helped 'realign', there was no longer any question – it was real. It was also fair to say that Marjorie had underestimated the depth of their grudge against robots, of any kind. She arrived at her former place of work to find a scene of absolute, wonderful chaos.

Beaumont Street, generally serene with its orderly flow of pod-traffic, was complete gridlock. Pod-cars littered both sides of the street and the cacophony of electronic warnings emanating from each of them was deafening.

There were people everywhere – some looked confused, some strangely satisfied and others were pulsating with anger. 'Outrageous!' a tall, garrulous businessman yelled into his mobile watch. 'I want to speak to a human being this instant. Where the hell is my pod?! It's 20 minutes late. I'm going to miss my train!'

The general state of pandemonium had brought most of the Randolph's guests out to have a look. The concierge was screaming at the solitary constable. 'I won't have it,' he shouted, 'our VIP guests were awakened at 6:24 by these bloody cars! Can't you turn them off?!"

Constable Miller was one of just three city policeman left, and there seemed very little he could do. All around him, a sea of pod-cars had brought traffic to a standstill. Each one was loudly hailing a previous occupant but no one seemed interested in collecting their belongings. He took a photo with his mobile watch and sent it up to headquarters. Then he spoke into a collar microphone, dictating his full report. He was just beginning to take statements from a few witnesses when his watch vibrated. 'Constable Miller,' he answered. 'What's that? You're joking. Broad Street too? Well, it's a complete shambles here. Backed up all the way past St Giles now.' He paused and listened. 'Are you telling me this is city-wide? Well, you better get someone on the phone from the pod-car companies. What do you mean no-one's answering?!'

But of course no one was.

Robotitech's headquarters, every pod-car manufacturer for that matter, employed an automated help line. Unfortunately, this situation wasn't covered by the standard pre-recorded options. Bill and his fellow council leaders came scurrying out of the building and stared in panicked disbelief; career-ending headlines flitted across their minds. It wouldn't look good for senior leadership given that traffic and transport fell under their remit. Perhaps they'd run things a little too lean.

But still nobody noticed Marjorie sitting on the steps of the former Ashmolean, wearing a bemused expression. She glanced at the Lifebook posts on her watch – someone had posted: – What will Marj do next?!

– Don't know. Looking for ideas?

In swift succession, a number of replies appeared along with constructive suggestions; friends posted places to visit, books to read, a pet sanctuary in need of new volunteers. But one in particular caught her attention. It was from 'Andy', the first IT specialist she'd had to 'realign'. A talented young man who had programmed countless machines and found his own job axed right after he trained a robot to do the programming. He would have been suicidal if it wasn't for Marjorie, who discovered his passion for singing. Now he was the lead in a rock band.

– Sending u tix to our next gig. Looks like you found your calling!

– Thanks! But not sure I follow. My calling...?

– Your pod-car traffic jam idea's gone viral! You're a rebel.

- Me?
- Yeah you! How can we help? Every
robot has a weakness you know.

Marjorie was a rule follower. She survived. That's what had
got her this far in life. *Which was where exactly?* Overweight,
divorced and unemployed. She surveyed the scene around
her. The noise, the bleeping, the shouting, the hand gestures.
She breathed in deeply and the chaos tickled her nose. This
was better than cake. Better than wine. She texted back:

How about a little wilful obstruction...?!

The Census Enumerator

GEOFF BREMBLE

Dawn on the 2nd of April 1861 promised a bright if somewhat cold early spring day, and it was 8.00 am when the Census Enumerator set off to record the lives of the 270 people living on Beaumont Street. It had been a few days earlier when he had been given this, one of the plum streets in Oxford, as part of his route. He imagined it being inhabited by intelligent, refined and generally courteous people, and maybe a few so-called artisans. But even they would be somewhat higher up the rung of the class system than those he had interviewed 10 years previously. The 1851 census was the first one he had done and he had been given a route that included the terraced houses that bordered the Oxford Canal and whose inhabitants had a propensity to be careless with the truth when answering his questions. Some of them had been of an age when they couldn't remember, or had never known their birth date. But what he really hadn't been able to excuse was their casual attitude to providing information and not seeming to understand the importance of the census exercise.

His route started with the houses opposite St Mary Magdalen church with the interviews passing off without incident, although the inhabitants of the houses from numbers 7 to 10 did seem a bit surly or, if one was being kind, out of sorts. It was after he had turned into Beaumont Street that he began to have trouble; not outward aggression but definitely a simmering sense of dissatisfaction. The 'Heads' of the first four houses were, in chronological order: Mr Cousins, a Chemist aged 48, at No. 1; Mr Cox, a Shoemaker aged 59, at No. 2; Mr Searle, a Tailor aged 54, at No. 3; and Mr Leach, a Carver and Gilder, aged 38 at No. 4. All gave vent to feelings of being put upon but it was Mr Cox who voiced them most vociferously.

'It's a waste of time answering all these questions seeing as how we won't even be here in a few years from now,' were his opening remarks.

Startled at what he interpreted as being a suggestion of ill health, the Enumerator broke the sacred code of never engaging in conversation with the people they were interviewing. If truth be told he was a person who enjoyed a good gossip.

'Why, Mr Cox, are you not well?'

'No, I'm perfectly well, thank you. It's the money men and those in their ivory towers, that's not well,' he exploded.

'I don't understand,' responded the Enumerator politely.

'You don't understand, nor do I. Them idiots are going to build a huge hotel just where we're standing. It'll mean me and my daughters and a four-year-old child thrown out onto the streets and having to find somewhere else to live.'

'But I thought that was only a rumour?' questioned the Enumerator.

'It most certainly isn't. I have it on good authority it'll be built on this corner of Magdalen and Beaumont and of course they've chosen this spot because they think they can push the likes of us around. They could have built it anywhere else along the street, but no, that's where the money and the influence is. They didn't dare take them on and so it'll be the likes of us that gets thrown out.'

Mr Cox paused, but before the Enumerator could respond he started up again.

'If this Hotel is as big as I've heard there'll be people coming and going all day long, and night time too – nobody will be able to sleep. It's a beautiful road now, quiet with very few carriages moving down its length and with only the cattle on market days causing a mess. But that'll be nothing compared to what it'll be like from the horses and carriages of those what's coming to the Hotel after it's been opened, you mark my words.'

Mr Cox paused again but the Enumerator was so shocked by this vision of mayhem that he was rendered speechless. Mr Cox took the opportunity to start up again and finish off his tirade.

'And what's more, that bloody architect Wilkinson, he's been the one chosen to draw up the plans and, you know what, he lives two doors down at No. 5. I'll bet my shirt on it that they're not going to knock his house down, very convenient I calls it.'

The Enumerator, realising there was no arguing with Mr Cox, beat a hasty retreat and, having survived further protestations of indignation at Nos. 3 and 4, he reached No. 5. He was relieved to find that Mr Wilkinson was a most agreeable man and not at all put out by being interrupted while working on plans for his next project. The Enumerator decided it would not be a good idea to enquire as to what that might be.

The rest of his 'clients' responded to his questions in a

generally amicable way. They of course were in the upper echelons of the class system, or they thought they were, and were content to respond fully, on some occasions too fully, to the questions they were asked. On reflection, the Enumerator decided that he shouldn't have been surprised given that he had to deal with three 'Men of the Cloth', three Surgeons, three Merchants, six Fund-holders, two Land and House proprietors and a College Bed Maker. In addition there were three others who might be termed as being the cream of the crop. First and foremost there was a Mr William Brunner living at No. 11, Coroner of the City of Oxford; secondly there was an Architect, Mr Edward Bruton at No. 14 who had recently heard that he was about to be made a Fellow of the Royal Institute of Architects and who was building a reputation to challenge Mr Wilkinson's. As a result he was more than a bit miffed at not having been given the responsibility for what the Enumerator had decided to call Mr Cox's project. Finally, at No. 34 was a Mr Biddle who had recently heard that he was in the running to be invited to act as one of the solicitors who would help manage the project.

It was two years later, in early spring 1863, that the Enumerator came upon an announcement whilst browsing through the *Oxford Times*.

Randolph Hotel, Beaumont Street, Oxford
Bankers – Messrs Parsons, Thomson and Old Bank
Solicitors – Messrs Morrell, Biddle and Hawkins
Architect – Mr William Wilkinson

This first-class hotel is intended for accommodation of families and gentlemen visiting and staying for a time in Oxford.

This hotel will be built on the site at the corner of Beaumont Street, opposite Taylor and Randolph buildings and Martyrs Memorial.

This site includes the houses and premises occupied by Messrs. Thornton, Simmons, Richardson, Gardner, and Cousins in Magdalen Street; and Messrs Cousins, Cox, Searle, and Leach in Beaumont Street; the fees simple of which have been secured by the promoters; and it will perhaps fairly convey some idea of the extent of this valuable property, when it is stated that it contains an equal area (to within a few yards) to that of the great Grosvenor Hotel, Pimlico.

The importance of this site is scarcely to be overestimated; the immense frontage; the openness and airiness of the situation; the central position; the proximity of the business parts of the city and principal public buildings, and its command of the whole north of Oxford, including the rapidly increasing residential estates of Walton and Norham Manors, and Parktown, and the ready access to the Railway Stations, all tend to give the promoters a certainty of success.

The promoters are confident that the proposed Hotel will create an ample custom for itself without damage to the existing hotels in the city, and be the means of drawing many visitors to Oxford; and they are glad to state that they are receiving a large and increasing support from all quarters.

At a meeting of the promoters held on Wednesday last.

It was resolved to raise the sum of £40,000 to carry out the undertaking.

That £30,000 should be raised by 1500 shares of £20 each and £10,000 on debentures or other security.

The sum of £10,000 has been already guaranteed on the debentures, and a large proportion of the shares has been applied for by promoters in the University, City and neighbourhood.

Pending the publication of the prospectus containing the names of the Directors and Officers of the Company, which will appear in due course, those who wish to take shares in the undertaking can apply to Messrs Morrell, Biddle and Hawkins, solicitors.

The Enumerator smiled to himself and murmured, 'The old bugger was right. I wonder where he is now. He must have had good contacts, but I suppose being a Shoemaker he'd have had some very interesting clients and could have learnt from them all he needed to know about what was going on.'

Meanwhile, the old bugger himself was reading the same announcement and thinking about his rant to the Enumerator just over two years previously.

'I told you so,' he muttered to himself.

Three years later on Tuesday the 13th of February 1866 the Enumerator spotted a piece in the *Oxford Mail* regarding a dinner to be held that day at the newly built Randolph Hotel. It was to celebrate its opening, and over 200 of Oxford's finest had been invited. He still remembered the day he had been given an inkling of what had now transpired, and wondered if Mr Cox and his fellow travellers would be invited to attend. He decided to go down to Beaumont Street an hour or so before the dinner was due to start, hoping to find out if they had been. The evening sky was clear of cloud and he wrapped himself up well in order to keep out the cold. As he made his way through Oxford he was careful to keep to the pavements wherever possible, the roads having been churned up by the traffic during the three years of the building of the Hotel.

He was now standing on the University Museum steps immediately opposite the Hotel entrance, and had been there for about 20 minutes when the first diners started arriving in their carriages. Suddenly he became aware of a stream of people going into the Taylor Institute at the St Giles Street end of the Museum. Most of them went directly in but one figure detached himself and came and stood near to him. He too seemed to be watching the diners but the Enumerator couldn't quite make out his face. The man eventually turned towards him and he recognised him instantly.

'Mr Cox,' he called out, 'Mr Cox, how are you?'

The man turned and walked over to him.

'I'm sorry young man, you have the advantage over me.'

'Mr Cox, don't you remember me? I was the Census Enumerator who interviewed you five years ago. It was you who told me that this Hotel was going to happen and here it is now. What do you think of it?'

'Yes, I do remember you and I clearly remember having a good rant about it. I hope I wasn't too hard,' Mr Cox responded with a grin, 'but to answer your question, while I agree that it's a magnificent building, and that in an odd way I feel quite proud of it, I can assure you, you won't ever find me going inside.'

'I suppose not, given how badly they treated you. But wouldn't you like to have just a little look, even if you don't partake of the food and drink that's on offer?'

'Well maybe just a peek, but not any more than that,' was the response.

'I think you really should, after all you and your family have been uprooted by its being built. But more importantly, how are your family and where are you living now?'

'In George Street,' Mr Cox responded,' with my daughter, and before you ask me, I've given up Shoes. I'm now a Book-maker, not as physical as making shoes but just as satisfying and my daughter is assisting me as my Book-binder.'

'Well, I'm so pleased to see that you're still around and healthy, and it must be a pleasure working with someone that close to you,' the Enumerator offered before continuing, 'by the way I'm intrigued as to what you were doing coming over from the Institute at this time of day.'

'Still with the questions I see, you can't stop asking them can you? Well, as you have asked, I'll tell you – I'm attending a drawing class, it's due to start in about thirty minutes. I've always enjoyed a bit of drawing, and when I saw this course advertised I said to myself, Why not? You might learn something, even at your age. So here I am two days a week for two hours each day and it's only costing me eight shillings a month, and as I see it that's money well spent.'

'That's very interesting, put on by the University is it?'

'No, nothing to do with them. The idea is that art can help people who produce things, such as my shoes, look at things more deeply, thus enabling them to make their products more appealing to customers.'

'So it's just for people like you?'

'No, they also think that it can take people to a happier and more useful life and so anyone who has a mind can attend,' responded Mr Cox before finishing with a smile, 'even you. Anyway, enough of me, may I ask you a question: What are you doing here?'

'It's the inaugural dinner for the opening of the Hotel and I thought I'd come down to see who might be going,' said the Enumerator before adding with a grin, 'I can see that you've not been invited. But what about the others who had to leave, do you keep in touch with any of them? I see No. 4 is still standing so presumably Mr Leach is still there?'

'Well that's where you'd be wrong, he and his family moved to Queen Street and a Mrs Symmonds is living there now. She and her son have been given the responsibility of managing the Hotel's stables. And see those huts, between the Hotel and No. 5, the ones the builders have been using? Well that's where the stables will be after the huts have been demolished. But in between times I've no idea what they're going to do with the undoubtedly large number of carriages that will arrive at their door, never mind the horses. What's more somebody's going to have to do something about the state of the roads. The visitors they're hoping to attract won't put up with having to wade around in three inches of mud every time they step out of their carriages.'

'Yes, you're right and I think we're about to get some idea of what it'll be like. Take a look down there,' said the Enumerator pointing to the Worcester College end of the street.

The two of them peered into the gloom of the evening and watched the approaching carriages already starting to clog up the street with the inevitable confrontations between drivers looking for a safe, clean space to offload their passengers.

'There's a few more coming from St Giles,' observed Mr

Cox, before adding with more than a touch of pleasure in his voice, 'chaos, absolute chaos!'

'Now then Mr Cox, you shouldn't be taking pleasure in other people's discomfort and so I think we should go back to the conversation we seem to have drifted away from. We'd covered you and Mr Leach and we're left with Mr Cousins and Mr Searle, so maybe we can take Mr Cousins first.'

'Yes, maybe we should. Well he's landed on his feet; been appointed as the Hotel's chemist and they've set him up with a shop in the Hotel and on the back of that he's been able to move his family into a big house on the Banbury Road.'

'I'm not surprised, he struck me as a very astute man when I interviewed him. So what about Mr Searle? He seemed to have a thriving business which, as far as I can see, has now closed down.'

'It has, but I'm not sure what's happened to him except that I know he found God and moved to London; calls himself a Scripture Reader now, whatever that is.'

'That's a surprise but, as they say, God works in mysterious ways.' The Enumerator paused, then continued, 'there's one more thing I must ask you: Mr Wilkinson at No. 5? I interviewed him immediately after interviewing you and he seemed a most likable man, but I'm not sure that you saw him that way.'

'You're correct in thinking that but I have to admit he was a good neighbour, apart from you know what, and I suppose if he hadn't done the job somebody else would have, so I don't bear him any grudges.'

'I'm pleased about that and you're right, there'd have been plenty of architects more than willing to take his place – Mr Bruton for one – remember him from No. 14,' responded the

Enumerator who was now stamping his feet in an attempt to get some warmth into them.

'I do indeed. I didn't really know him but I've heard that he's moved to a house on the Woodstock Road. I understand that he's conducting his business from there while also teaching three young men to become architects, one can only assume that he must be well on the way to making a name for himself.'

It was just at that moment that the Enumerator spotted the door to No. 5 opening.

'Look,' he said pointing to the two figures coming out of the house, 'one of them must be Mr Wilkinson, but I'm not sure who the other one is. Can you see?'

'Yes, and you're right, it is Mr Wilkinson. Presumably he is going to the dinner. The other's the Reverend Tyrwhitt if I'm not mistaken; you must know him, Vicar of Magdalen church.'

There was a pause as they watched the two men moving towards the entrance to the Hotel. The Enumerator then made a suggestion.

'Let's go over, see if we can get you inside.'

'No,' protested Mr Cox, 'I told you, I don't need to see the inside of it.'

'Well I think you do, so come on,' responded the Enumerator, who was already walking towards the two figures, with which Mr Cox reluctantly followed him.

'Mr Wilkinson,' shouted the Enumerator, waving his arms as he crossed the road, and narrowly missing being run down by a carriage and four, 'can we have a word with you?'

Mr Wilkinson turned in surprise and paused as he tried to identify who was hailing him and then, not recognising the figure, he turned his attention to the second man. By this time Mr Cox had caught up with him and was offering his hand; it was then that he recognised who it was.

'Good evening Mr Cox this is a surprise. What can I do for you?' he said as he took the proffered hand.

It was the Enumerator who responded to this question.

'He wonders if he could just have a quick look inside the Hotel; not for long, just for a few minutes.'

Mr Wilkinson paused before responding.

'I'm afraid that won't be possible on this occasion. As you can see, the Reverend Tyrwhitt and I are heading for the inaugural dinner celebrating the opening of the Hotel.'

It was then that the Enumerator pressed his point.

'May I remind you gentlemen that if the Hotel hadn't been built Mr Cox would still have been your neighbour. It seems to me extremely unfair that neither Mr Cox nor Mr Searle nor Mr Leach nor Mr Cousins have been invited to attend; after all they've had much upheaval in their lives as a consequence of it being built.'

There was an embarrassed silence, broken by the Reverend Tyrwhitt as he turned to Mr Wilkinson.

'William, I'm sure no one would be offended if you invited Mr Cox to come in with us and have a look round the entrance hall, just for a few minutes.'

He turned to Mr Cox, 'Would that be alright with you Sir?'

'Yes, I think I would like that,' responded the now somewhat flustered Mr Cox.

'Then that's settled. Yes William?' said the Reverend turning towards Mr Wilkinson whose face immediately broke into a smile.

'It seems that I've been outmanoeuvred by a gentleman I feel I ought to know but cannot recall in what way, and by the good Reverend here. Yes, come on Mr Cox, let's go inside, but only for a quick look, and I would be delighted if you and your family would join me and the Reverend for tea and scones at some later date.'

He then turned to the Enumerator,

'Much as I would like to invite you in as well, I think that might be overdoing it; but thank you for giving me the opportunity to make amends in some small way for the upheaval I seem to have caused in Mr Cox's life.'

'That's perfectly alright and I thank you for your understanding but, if I may, I would just like to have a quick word with Mr Cox before you go in.'

He then turned to his new-found friend,

'Mr Cox, I think I'll be off now, I'm getting a bit cold standing out here. It's been nice to catch up again and can I thank you for indulging my curiosity as to what happened to you and the others. So I'll bid you farewell but I'll be sure to look out for you when I'm in town, and I might even join you in your drawing classes or call round for a new pair of shoes, you never know.'

'It's been a pleasure,' responded Mr Cox as the two of them shook hands, 'and thank you for bullying me into the Hotel – I wouldn't have done it on my own.'

'Happy to have been of service,' responded the Enumerator who then started to walk towards St Giles. A few yards on he stopped and looked back to where he saw Mr Cox, followed by Mr Wilkinson and the Reverend Tyrwhitt, mounting the steps to the Hotel and disappearing inside.

'Well I think that's my good deed for the day,' he said to

himself as he walked on, a satisfied smile lighting up his face.

A blue plaque dedicated to William Wilkinson was unveiled on the front of 5 Beaumont Sreet in October 2016 by Revd Professor William Whyte, tutorial fellow in history at St John's College